"Who are you?"

Sean stared intently into Mac's eyes. "My husband was a rogue, my marriage a sham. Yet here you are, the same man, but completely different. It seems unreal. It seems like a lie, but a wonderful one."

The same man. That was the lie. "Forget the past, Sean. Let's just start from the beginning and discover each other again."

"I don't know. We're *married*. We've been through this. It's never worked between us."

To be married to Sean was all Mac wanted. But he wanted her to want *him*...the man he was, not the man she'd been married to before. He'd make her forget the lies, deceit, the other women. He'd make her want him in a way she'd never wanted her husband—the man she thought he was.

ABOUT THE AUTHOR

Mary Anne Wilson lives in Southern California with her husband, three children, two exceptional grandchildren and an odd assortment of dysfunctional pets. She has been a Rita Award finalist for outstanding romantic suspense, makes regular appearances on the Waldenbooks bestseller list and has been a Reviewer's Choice nominee for *Romantic Times* magazine. She believes real love is a rare and precious gift—the greatest mystery in life.

Books by Mary Anne Wilson

HARLEQUIN AMERICAN ROMANCE
495—HART'S OBSESSION

Don't miss any of our special offers. Write to us at the following address for information on our newest releases.

Harlequin Reader Service
P.O. Box 1397, Buffalo, NY 14240
Canadian address: P.O. Box 603,
Fort Erie, Ont. L2A 5X3

MARY ANNE WILSON

WILSON

COULD IT BE YOU?

Harlequin Books

TORONTO • NEW YORK • LONDON
AMSTERDAM • PARIS • SYDNEY • HAMBURG
STOCKHOLM • ATHENS • TOKYO • MILAN
MADRID • WARSAW • BUDAPEST • AUCKLAND

To Mary Ellen O'Neill, for her support,
imagination and good taste in movies. Thanks.

ISBN 0-373-16523-4

COULD IT BE YOU?

Prologue

Mackenzie Gerard sat on the side of his lower bunk, on a lumpy mattress that barely covered the sagging springs. The pungency of disinfectant was everywhere, but it couldn't quite hide the lingering staleness left by all the people who had passed through this place before him. People who had stared at the same dull green walls marred by obscenities, people who had paced the stained cement floor, people who had wanted out.

It had taken just two short days for his nerves to become ragged. He needed to sleep, but couldn't. Raking his hands through his hair, he took a deep breath and glanced at the three men who had come in after him. Derelicts, drunks, petty crooks. They'd all been reduced to sleeping on the floor with a thin blanket and a single pillow.

He shook his head. He'd been in rotten places before, in bad situations, but this time he'd hit bottom.

Mac stood and crossed to the bars that fronted the twelve-by-sixteen-foot jail cell. The glassed-in briefing rooms were directly across from him, and as he rested his forearms on the cross bars, he saw a reflection of himself through the bars.

At six feet, he was lean and hard from years of manual labor on docks up and down the East Coast and in the Gulf. His Levi's were torn from use, not fashion's dictates, and his hands were callused. His skin was tanned from working outside, and with a full mustache, a three-day beard, and his thick black hair long enough to brush the shoulders of his faded work shirt, he looked like what he was—a man who'd fought to survive, any way he had to.

The sound of a metal door opening at the end of the corridor drew his attention, and Mac saw one of the guards coming toward the holding cells.

"Gerard?" he called out.

Mac lifted his hand. "Here."

The guard motioned for Mac to step back. Then he opened the door and said, "Come on. You're out of here."

He didn't have to repeat himself. Mac quickly stepped out of the cell into the corridor and followed the guard back through the open door. They went down a short hallway and into a small side room.

A counter ran along the back wall, and a policewoman was behind it, backed by what looked like a storage area. The guard stepped past Mac and spoke to the woman. "Release. Gerard, Mackenzie."

The policewoman flipped through a stack of papers in front of her, then took out two and slid them over to Mac. "Read these and sign them," she said in a monotone. "By signing them, you agree to make your court appearance on the above date, and you agree to stay within the jurisdiction of the court until resolution of this case. In the event you do not appear on the said date, a bench warrant will be issued for your arrest. Any questions?''

"No."

She handed him a pen. "Then sign on the bottom line."

Mac scrawled his name on the paper, not really caring what it said, as long as signing it got him out of there. He went through the rest of the release procedure in less than ten minutes, and was escorted to the exit. He stepped out onto a side street, into a June night.

New Orleans was alive with sounds and activity. The tang of the nearby water mingled with the aroma of spicy foods and the scent of the city itself. Music played in the distance, but Mac barely noticed it.

He pushed his hands into the pockets of his jeans and headed toward the center of town. He was free. He walked faster, wishing he'd walked like this last week, when he'd found out three of the men on his crew were stealing from the owner of the warehouse where he worked. He could have hopped a freighter and been halfway to Brazil by now.

He rounded a corner and headed down toward the docks, and the boardinghouse where he'd been staying for the past four months. Since the days when he'd run away from a string of foster homes, he'd held onto one rule—don't get involved, just get out. It had worked for over twenty years, and it was still valid.

In less than an hour, Mac had left the boardinghouse with everything he owned in a worn duffel bag slung over his shoulder. He started up the narrow street away from the docks and toward the main route out of New Orleans.

He never once looked back.

Chapter One

Seattle, Washington, July 2

Mac had been walking for about an hour, ever since the truck driver had left him just outside the city. He'd made his way past residential areas and upscale businesses until a misting rain began to fall, and then he'd entered a dreary section of the city, near the water. A dilapidated clock tower read 1:00 a.m.

Small stores and businesses lined the hilly streets. They were all shut tight, their hissing neon lights casting garish shadows in the night. As Mac walked the silent streets, he moved closer to the curb to avoid groups of homeless people who had set up camp in front of closed and abandoned buildings.

The persistent mist brushed his skin with coolness, and his denim jacket was beginning to feel damp on his shoulders. Shifting his duffel bag to his other hand, he inhaled deeply. He knew he couldn't be more than a mile from the dock area.

Once he found the docks, he'd find a place to stay dry until the early shifts started, and then he'd go looking for a position on a crew where they didn't ask any questions. He'd take anything, as long as they were shipping out in the next day or so.

He picked up his pace as he crested a hill and saw Puget Sound. A scattering of lights at the end of the street seemed to frame the dark blur of water beyond. As the rain increased, Mac started down the steep street.

Halfway down, the rain turned into a torrent, as if the heavens had opened up. He tugged his watch cap lower on his dark hair, tucked his chin into the collar of his worn jacket and took off down the street at a jog looking for cover.

He could barely see far enough ahead to make out the crisscross of overpasses at the foot of the street, and a stretch of dark buildings. But just before the corner on the other side of the street, he saw lights through the rain. Red and blue neon flashed *The Belly Up Bar & Grill* through the sheeting rain.

Ducking his head, he took off at a run and cut across the slick pavement, and just as a huge clap of thunder shook the night he reached the doorway to the bar. Muffled strains of honky-tonk music could be heard from behind the scarred wooden doors, and even before he went inside Mac knew it would be like a lot of places he'd gone into before—a place to stay for a few hours, a drink, and shelter from the elements.

He pushed back the door and was met by stuffy heat, smoke-filled air, country music on the jukebox, and the drone of conversation from a dozen or so customers. A few men who looked like dockworkers occupied the row of booths to the right, a couple in the poolroom at the back were in the middle of a game, and one man sitting at the bar to the left of the doors slouched over his beer.

Mac skimmed off his cap and tucked it in his pocket, then headed across the tiled floor to the bar. He pushed his damp duffel bag between the brass footrail and the front of the bar. Then he slipped onto a stool and undid his jacket.

"What'll it be?"

Mac glanced toward the bartender, a burly man with tattoos decorating both beefy arms, the pictures dancing as he polished glasses at the far end of the bar.

"Draft," Mac said as he raked his fingers through his damp hair. His eyes met his own gaze in the smoky mirrors that lined the back of the bar.

His hair had grown long enough to go past his shoulders, and not shaving since he'd left New Orleans had left him with a thick, dark beard that hid most of his face. A stranger. Someone few people would notice. And once he was out of the country, Mackenzie Gerard would be a minor footnote to a case in the files of the New Orleans district attorney's office.

As the bartender set the frosty mug of beer in front of him, Mac fumbled in his pocket and tossed two bills on the counter. That left him about five dollars. But with any luck, he'd soon have a berth on a ship out of here, and he wouldn't need American money for a long time. As he lifted the mug to take a drink, the entry doors opened, and for a moment Mac felt the rush of cold air. Then the doors snapped shut, closing out the night and the storm.

Mac took a long drink of his beer, and the next thing he knew something struck him in the shoulder, sending the beer sloshing over the sides of the mug. It ran over his hand and down onto the bar. "Damm it," Mac muttered as he set the mug on the counter and reached for a napkin.

"Sorry, sorry," someone muttered thickly, as the stool next to Mac was snatched back from the bar.

Mac wiped his hand, then laid the napkin on the counter before he glanced briefly to his right. He had an impression of a man unsteady after too much to drink, trying to sit on the high stool.

"Shame to waste good beer," the man muttered as he sat forward and hit the bar with the flat of his hand. "More beer for my friend, bartender, and a double whiskey for me."

The last thing Mac wanted or needed was to become a drinking buddy to some bum. "You don't have to—"

The man cut him off. "Yes, I do."

Mac took a good look at the stranger and knew he definitely wasn't a bum. No bum wore a well-cut trench coat darkened by the rain, or had immaculately clean hands, or perfectly styled black hair combed straight back from a clean-shaven face flushed from the effects of too much alcohol.

When the bartender set another mug in front of Mac, he didn't fight it. He took it as the bartender cleared away the old beer. "Thanks," he said to the stranger. "I appreciate it."

The man gave him a nod, then held up his own glass in a salute. In one shot, he tossed the amber liquid to the back of his throat and put the glass back down with a cracking thud. "Another," he called to the bartender.

Mac took a drink from his beer, then glanced at the stranger in the mirror behind the bar. He definitely didn't fit in here, but as Mac watched the man toss back another double whiskey, he had the strangest feeling that he'd met him before. God knew he'd met enough people in his wanderings, but he seldom brushed up against people like this man.

The stranger met Mac's gaze in the reflection. The alcohol was giving his face a puffiness at his eyes and jaw. "Name's Elliot, Charles Elliot," he said.

Mac took another sip of beer. "I'm Mac."

"Mac." The man nodded to him in the reflection of the mirror. He shivered and pushed his empty glass toward the bartender again. "I forgot how wet this place could be."

Mac sipped some of the cool liquid, then sat back. "I wouldn't know."

The man eyed Mac in the smoky mirrors. "I *do* know. I know all too well. And I should have stayed in France." He ran a hand over his face. "But I needed to come back to take care of some business. Then the flight was later than it was suppose to be, and I missed the last ferry out. Too late to do much else but wait for the next ferry." He reached for the fresh drink the bartender pushed in front of him.

"You're waiting for a ferry?"

"That's the only way to get to the island. Sanctuary Island."

Sanctuary Island. Mac closed his eyes for a moment, then stared down at the foaming beer in his mug. What a name. Sanctuary. He wasn't given to flights of fantasy, never had been, but for a split second he wished he was running to a place like that, rather than to a freighter. He took a long drink of the beer, then leaned on the bar with his elbows. "Thanks again for the beer," he said.

"The least I could do," Elliot said. "Have another." He raised his hand to get the bartender's attention. "Give my friend another beer."

"No, I've had enough. I need to—"

"You *need* another."

The idea of going out in the rain wasn't at all appealing. "Maybe one more."

"Good. That's my philosophy. One more. I came in to fortify myself before sitting in the car at the landing waiting for the early ferry. A bit of whiskey makes things more tolerable. Hedonistic, I know, but it's true."

"Whatever," Mac murmured as he took the fresh beer.

"My wife always preaches moderation...in all things. Not too much to drink, not too much partying, not too much indulgence, not too much fun." He laughed—it was a brittle sound—and lifted his glass in a salute. "To overindulgence, to fun, to partying, to good drink, and to Sean."

"Sean?" Mac asked.

"My wife. Sean Warren-Elliot. Daughter and only child of Louis Warren, founder of Warren International. Ever heard of them?"

Mac knew the name from stamps on crates on the loading docks he'd worked on over the years. "Sure. Import-export. You married into that?"

Elliot's expression seemed to tighten, the slackness from the alcohol offset by an intense frown for a moment before it was gone. He sipped more whiskey, then exhaled on a hiss. "You're drinking with the vice president of sales for Europe. And I own a hefty block of stock."

"It sounds as if you're set," Mac murmured.

"You know how it is—rich in assets, poor in cash. Story of my life until now." He finished off the last of his drink, but didn't ask for another. He stared at the empty glass for a long moment, then said, "Marrying the boss's daughter doesn't automatically give you money. You have to figure that out all on your own."

Mac finished off his beer, the alcohol blurring the edges of life and the rainy night. "It sounds as if you're doing all right." He glanced at the man. "That coat must have set you back plenty."

He shrugged as he finished his whiskey. "Five hundred. French fashion. You have to keep up appearances. Even Sean agrees to that. She's the last word in keeping up appearances." He laughed harshly, then took a wallet out of an inside pocket in the coat and laid a large bill on the bar.

Mac caught a glimpse of a row of credit cards in the wallet, and facing them was a photo of a woman with long blond hair that fell in a pale veil around slender shoulders. Delicate bone structure accentuated high cheekbones, a vaguely sharp chin, and full, pale lips. When he caught the expression in the huge amber eyes, he felt taken aback. There was neither joy nor anger there, just a certain sense of detachment. A coolness that made his skin tingle.

"Sean?" he asked.

Elliot glanced at the photo, then flipped the wallet shut before he pushed it into his pocket. "Yeah, Sean. For some reason, her old man called her by a boy's name. I haven't seen Sean for nine months, but I'll vouch for the fact that she's no boy."

Mac looked at Elliot, that feeling of having seen him before coming back so strongly that it added to the goose bumps on his skin. One thing he knew for sure, this man really did have everything, including a beautiful wife named Sean. But how could he have been away from her for so long? "Nine months is a long time."

"I've been kept busy in Europe." He slid off the seat and had to balance himself with one hand on the back of the stool. "But I'm back now, and I'm ready to set things right. As soon as the ferry service starts up again, I'll do that very thing."

Mac finished off the rest of his beer, then turned and looked up at Elliot, who was doing up the buttons of his trench coat. When the alcohol-blurred eyes looked up, the tingling at his neck turned into an eerie sensation that ran over his nerves. The eyes. Blue eyes. And he knew why he'd thought he'd seen this man before. It was as if Mac were looking in a mirror, a mirror that reflected a distorted image of himself.

He shook his head. The idea of this man mirroring any part of him was ridiculous, but he couldn't rid himself of it, even by narrowing his eyes and trying to refocus. It only intensified his first reaction. *He* could be Charles Elliot, or might have been, if he'd had tons of money and a life that floated around him rather than ramming him head-on.

Take away the expensive clothes, the perfectly styled hair... Mac stared at the man's hands as they smoothed the front of his trench coat. Perfectly manicured hands, without scars or calluses. No rings, but still hands of privilege. The man didn't have Mac's beard or his long hair, he didn't have his rough clothes or his leaner build, but if he did . . .

Mac had heard that everyone had a double in this world, but he hadn't expected to find his in this dive, in Seattle, a city he'd never been in before in his life. And he hadn't expected to find that his double had the world by the tail, when all he had was a handful of nothing.

He looked down at his own hands, at the calluses that were etched on the pads of his palms and fingers. Hard work had torn them up, stamping them with the effort it had taken to survive. He and Elliot had lived at the opposite ends of the spectrum of life, he thought.

Beer rose bitterly in his throat as he clenched his hands into fists, then stood and spoke to the bartender. "Can you tell me how to get to where they'd be hiring crews for ships heading out?"

"Yeah, hang a left at the corner, and about a mile down you'll find the employment offices. When they open they can tell you who's hiring and where they're going."

"Thanks," Mac said, tugging his jacket together. Then he reached for his duffel bag.

"Hey, I'm heading that way," Elliot said. "The ferry dock's just past it. I'll give you a lift."

Mac faced Elliot, who matched his own six feet exactly. "If it's not too much trouble."

"None at all," the man mumbled, then headed for the entrance.

Mac tugged on his watch cap as he followed him out of the bar. A foghorn bellowed in the Sound, and as its mournful cry died out, Mac realized the only noises

were the rain hitting the pavement and a hissing sound
from the neon lights above the bar.

Rain beat on the sidewalk and ran down the street.
No one was in sight, and Mac figured all sane people
were inside, safe and dry and in bed. He took a deep
breath of the pungent air, which was filled with the
tang of the nearby water and the odors of the street.

He stepped out onto the sidewalk and saw Elliot just
ahead of him. The man crossed to the curb, and he
staggered as he stepped down onto the street, almost
missing his footing. He grabbed at a parking sign,
steadied himself, then stepped out onto the blacktop
of the street.

Mac hurried after him and called out, "Hey, Elliot,
why don't you let me drive?"

The man stopped and turned. Standing in the middle of the street, he looked at Mac, the rain streaming
off his face and the neon lights splashing him with
garish colors. He gave a stupid grin as he fumbled in
his coat pocket, then tossed a ring of keys toward Mac.

As Mac stepped off the curb to catch the keys that
arced through the rainy night, he heard the screech of
tires as brilliant lights came around the corner. For a
split second he saw Elliot's face frozen in the light, the
slack look of drunkenness stark in the glare. As his
fingers closed over the keys, Mac realized this was all
wrong. There was no way the car could stop. He
screamed at Elliot at the same time he twisted and
dove for the sidewalk.

The world altered in that moment. Normal time
changed to slow motion as Mac felt himself hurdle
through the rain and night, stopped by a jarring impact to his head. The smell of burning rubber and rain-

soaked concrete filled his nostrils, and the sound of screeching brakes echoed all around. Mac tasted grit in his mouth, gulped in air, then pushed against the sidewalk with both hands and forced himself to his knees.

The world spun and faltered. Mac looked up as rain beat against his face. He could see the red glow of taillights being swallowed up in the dark of the hilly street. He twisted to look for Elliot. For a moment he couldn't see a thing, but then he spotted a dark heap in the middle of the street. It could have been a pile of discarded clothes, but he knew it wasn't.

There was a roaring in his head, and he didn't know if it was a motor or himself screaming. Pain was everywhere as he staggered to his feet. He almost fell back to his knees, but then he caught himself, gained his balance and pushed himself to his feet.

Mac staggered toward where Elliot lay on the road, the rain running around the inert body, then dropped to his knees. Grabbing a handful of trench coat, he managed to roll the man over onto his back.

His face was torn and bleeding, and his eyes were staring blindly upward into the torrential rain. Even before Mac touched the throat where the coat parted and felt no pulse, he knew the man was dead.

Mac was only vaguely aware of rain soaking him to the bone, or of the grinding pain in his head. All he could think of was that the man he'd talked to moments ago was dead. A man who could have been his other half, his alter ego, his twin, was gone, as if he had never existed. And it could have been Mac lying there dead in the rain. It could have been his life— snuffed out like a useless cigarette.

Mac let go of his hold on the trench coat, and Elliot's body slumped limply to one side. The man who had had everything was gone. Mac felt his hand tighten around the forgotten car keys. He looked down, opening his callused hand to stare at the keys. There was a rental tag on one of them, and there was a small black box on the leather ring.

Everything was nothing now. Nothing. That was exactly what Mac had, dead or alive. Nothing. If he had been Elliot, he would have everything. He closed his eyes, and the image of Elliot in the bar came to him with the sharpness of cutting glass. He could have been Elliot. He should have been. He should have been going home to a wife named Sean, to an island called Sanctuary, to a real life.

Sanctuary. Just the name shook him. His sanctuary. Despite the fuzziness and throbbing in his head, he suddenly knew that he wasn't going to go off into the night and back into the emptiness of running away. Quickly he reached into Elliot's inside pocket and took out his wallet. He pushed it in his jacket, then slipped his wallet out of his jeans and pushed it into Elliot's pocket.

As a siren sounded in the distance, someone yelled, "Hey, the cops are on their way!"

Mac looked up, saw the flashing of bright lights coming down the hill, cutting through the torrential rain and darkness, and staggered to his feet. No cops. No. He wasn't going back to New Orleans. He wasn't going to be locked up. He was going to disappear into a new life. He was going to Sanctuary Island.

He saw his duffel bag near the curb and almost went to pick it up, but he didn't. A man was coming out of the bar, and he knew he had to get out of here. Besides, the bag didn't belong to him anymore. He turned and saw the rental sedan Elliot had been heading for. Then, with a glance back at the bar, where the man was watching from the shelter of the entrance, he turned his back and took off at a jog for the rental car. He slipped the key in the lock, opened the door, then got inside, pushed the key into the ignition and started the car.

Without giving himself time to think, he put the car in gear and pulled away from the curb. He drove down and around the corner to the left, away from the blare of sirens and the blaze of lights, and left it all behind him.

He flipped on the headlights and the windshield wipers and kept glancing in the rearview mirror. But no lights or sirens came after him. God alone knew what the man at the bar had seen. But he couldn't do anything about that now. With a shaky sigh, he sank back in the seat and swiped at the wet hair clinging to his face. He drove south, past clusters of warehouses and darkened buildings, before he spotted the sign for the ferry landing.

The sign listed islands serviced by the ferries, and Sanctuary Island was at the bottom of the list. He turned at the arrow, slowly going down an incline to his right until a heavy chain with a red stop sign kept him from going farther. A large sign to the right of the chain gave ferry schedules, and in the glow of headlights through the rain blurred windshield Mac could read that the earliest ferry for Sanctuary Island left at 5:30 a.m. He glanced at the clock in the car. He had over three hours to wait.

The rain in his clothes was soaking through to his skin, and his hair was damp against his temples and neck. He swiped at his face and felt pain near his left temple. When he drew his hand back, he could see something dark on his fingers. He flipped off the headlights and the motor, then turned the dome light on and looked at his fingers. Blood.

Shifting forward, he looked at his reflection in the rearview mirror and was struck by how insane the past ten minutes had been. There was no way anyone would mistake him for Charles Elliot, not even someone who hadn't seen Elliot for nine months. Now, with an abrasion on his temple and blood running down his cheek into his beard, he looked like a derelict.

Carefully he took Elliot's wallet out of his pocket and flipped it open. The picture of Sean Elliot looked up at him, and he knew he should just put the wallet in an envelope and send it to the police. Then he'd ditch the car and get on the first freighter that would let him hire on.

But even as the thought came to him, the shriek of sirens cut through the stormy night. Mac quickly switched off the overhead light, then twisted in the seat and watched two police cars race by in the direction of the bar. The cops would be all over the place soon, and if he was on foot they'd stop him before he could go anywhere.

He turned in the seat and sank back against it, closing his eyes. He'd talked to the bartender and asked directions to the employment office. All they'd have to do is wait for him in the morning. They'd have him on charges that would make the ones in New Orleans look like child's play.

He tried to think, but his head was beginning to pound as if it had a life of its own, and the alcohol was making him drowsy. He was back to nothing. Again. But something in him wouldn't accept it. Not when he had a life within his grasp, and all he had to do was reach out and take it.

It might work, or it might not. But it was the best shot he had right now. Charles Elliot was going to Sanctuary Island. First, Mac had to clean up and make himself look like a man who had just come from France, not a down-on-his-luck drifter. He opened his eyes and started the car. As the windshield wipers brushed the rain away, the headlights caught the ferry schedule sign.

Sanctuary Island.

Mac stared at the sign as if it were an affirmation of what he was going to do. He was so tired of running, of going nowhere. He was going to Sanctuary Island.

He opened the wallet and counted eight twenty-dollar bills. Then he closed it and tossed it on the passenger seat, and with a glance in the rearview mirror he put the car in reverse and backed up the ramp, onto the street. Turning in the opposite direction from the bar, he drove to the first street, then swung left and up a hill. Near the top of the hill he saw what he needed— an all-night convenience store and gas station. He drove into the parking lot by the front of the store and turned off the engine and lights.

He saw a package of tissues on the console, and he took out a wad to wipe at his face. He soaked up the blood, grimacing at the contact with his wound. But he was able to clean most of the blood off his face and pull his cap low over his eyes.

Elliot's luggage was on the backseat, an overnight case and two large suitcases. Mac reached for the overnight bag and rested it on the console. Unzipping it, he found what he wanted—toiletries, clothes, shoes, underwear. The man could have lived out of the bag for a few days.

He put the bag on the floor in front, picked up the wallet and got out of the car and ran through the rain toward the store entrance. As he pushed back the glass doors and stepped into the starkly lit store, a man sorting cigarettes behind the counter looked up and frowned.

"Where do you keep your bandages?" Mac asked.

The man pointed to the back of the store to shelves near the drink cooler. "Back there."

Mac walked over to the display and picked out a pair of scissors, a box of gauze, disposable razors and some tape and disinfectant, then went back to the counter. He put his things down by the stacks of cigarettes, then spotted a display of maps by the register. He picked up one for Seattle and the islands in the Sound and added it to his pile.

The clerk silently rang up his purchases, then looked at him and said, "Ten dollars and sixty-two cents."

Mac flipped open Elliot's wallet and took out a twenty.

As the man made change, he frowned at Mac. "You all right, mister?"

"Sure. Just had an small accident." He looked right at the man. "Drank too much beer and forgot how to walk."

The man handed Mac his change. "Sure, mister."

"Do you have rest rooms here?"

The man turned and reached for a key tied by nylon rope to a hubcap that hung on the wall. "Out back. Bring back the key."

Mac took the hubcap and his bag and headed for the door. He ducked out into the storm and grabbed the overnight bag from the car. Then he hurried around to the rest rooms at the back of the building, where a single light barely illuminated the graffiti-scarred doors.

He unlocked the men's room and stepped into a six-by-eight space with one stall, a rusty sink, stained linoleum, and a stale, sour odor permeating the air.

Mac closed the door and went to the sink to look at his reflection in the cracked mirror on the wall. The abrasion and cut near his left temple was ragged and raw, but the bleeding had stopped. A tinge of purple surrounded the wound, and it looked slightly swollen.

Mac put the overnight case and the plastic bag on the short counter by the door and dug out the first-aid things. Quickly he cleaned the wound, put a gauze pad over it and secured it with tape. Then he stripped off his jacket, dropped it on the floor and opened the overnight bag.

Mac took out slightly mussed dark brown slacks, a beige V-necked cashmere pullover, socks, underwear, and the toiletry bag. Quickly he took off his shirt, tossed it on the wet jacket and got the scissors out of the bag. He laid out the scissors, along with shaving cream, razors and a brush-and-comb set, then started to put Mackenzie Gerard behind him.

In a short time, the man in the mirror had changed dramatically. Gone were the mustache, beard and long hair. Mac had trimmed his hair until it just touched his neck, and he combed it straight back from his face the way Elliot had. The slacks were well cut, and wearable with a belt that was tugged two notches tighter than it had been worn before. And the pullover felt incredibly soft after the roughness of the work shirt.

He ran a hand over his hair, then his clean-shaven jaw, and looked into the mirror. The man in the mirror could have been Charles Elliot, if Charles Elliot had been thinner, leaner, a bit more tanned, and with a more casual haircut. "Charles Elliot," he murmured.

He shivered suddenly, his stomach knotting from too much adrenaline. He turned from the mirror and quickly put on socks and the fine leather loafers. The shoes were a shade too tight, but bearable. He pulled a beige windbreaker out of the bag and slipped it on. Then he faced his reflection again.

"Charles Elliot," he said, with more conviction. A man with a future.

Chapter Two

It was a long shot, but Mac was going to take it. He repacked the bag, putting in the first-aid things and the scissors. He pushed the map into the pocket of his windbreaker.

As he turned, he all but tripped over his old clothes, which were lying on the floor. Without hesitating, he picked them up and pushed them into the trash can under the counter, disposing of a life that was past. He zipped up the jacket, then grabbed the overnight bag and the key on the hubcap and left.

The rain had stopped, and dawn was breaking. He tossed the overnight bag in the car, then went back into the store. He handed the clerk the key and said, "My friend told me to bring this in to you."

The man nodded and took the key without batting an eye. Mac felt a degree of relief that the man didn't recognize him. He was a different person from the man who had first arrived. When he got into the car, he exhaled with relief. He started the car, turned around and headed back to the ferry landing.

When he got there, a car was in line ahead of him, and he slipped in behind it, then killed the motor and

the lights. He turned on the dome light, took out the
wallet again and found Charles Elliot's driver's license.

At six feet, the man matched Mac in height, but he
outweighed Mac's one hundred and eighty pounds by
twenty pounds. His birthday made him two years
younger than Mac, who was thirty-five. The home
address was listed as Ten Look Out Point on Sanctuary Island. Mac looked through the rest of the wallet
and found over seven hundred dollars, a whole string
of credit cards, and a few business cards with Elliot's
name and the title Vice President of Sales, Warren International, on them.

The picture of Sean was one of five photos. One of
the others was fairly recent, a picture of Charles Elliot shaking hands with an older, gray-haired man,
both of them in tuxedos. The others were of formal
gatherings at which Charles Elliot seemed to have
taken center stage. Mac shifted in his seat and winced
at the headache pounding behind his eyes.

He laid the wallet on his thigh, then took out the
map and found Sanctuary Island on it. Look Out
Point was on the northern shore of the island, and
right on the water. He could find it in the morning,
when it was light, when his head didn't hurt so much
and things were clearer. Until then, he wanted nothing more than to rest.

He folded the map, laid it on the console and picked
up the wallet that held the picture of Sean Warren-
Elliot and put it in an inside pocket that rested against
his heart. He was so tired his body ached all over, and
it was a struggle to focus his eyes.

Closing his eyes, he settled against the seat. Rain beat on the car, and wind shook it, but Mac was warm and dry. And, at least for now, he had someplace to go. He thought of Sean Elliot as he slid into exhausted sleep. And someone would be waiting.

SEAN WOKE FROM SLEEP so abruptly that her heart pounded against her ribs and her breathing came in gulps. As the storm beat against the multipaned windows of the guest room at her father's home in Seattle, she forced herself to lie still in the cherry-wood canopy bed and open her clenched hands on the cool linen.

She had no idea why she had woken so suddenly or why she had such a feeling of dread coursing through her. Then she remembered. Pushing herself into a sitting position and leaning against the headboard, she felt the coldness of the wood through the thin silk of her short nightgown. She hugged her arms around herself. The meeting she'd left more than four hours before still haunted her.

"There's a real problem," Orin Quint of the accounting department at Warren International had told Sean and her father at the company's Seattle offices. The small, balding man had shuffled through papers in front of him, not looking at anyone, while he talked. "There's a shortfall in the accounts."

Sean had been the first to speak up. "Shortfall? What do you mean?"

Quint had stopped moving the papers, then met her gaze with his pale blue eyes. "There is over two million dollars missing from a variety of accounts."

Sean could still feel the sinking sensation in the pit of her stomach she'd experienced when he'd said that. Over two million. Gone. Lost somewhere. The meeting had gone on for two hours, while they tried to come up with some answers and some strategies. Two million plus. A drop in the bucket, compared to total revenues, but enough to cripple the company's share prices and reputation if the news got out.

She raked her fingers through her tangled blond hair, tucking it behind her ears, then rested her head against the headboard and stared at the storm through the windows. She felt as if the pins had been knocked out from under her, as if she had lost all control. And she hated that feeling, almost as much as she hated the feeling of being afraid.

A soft knock on the door echoed in the room. She heard her father's voice. "Sean?"

"Come in."

The door opened, letting the light from the hallway tumble into the room, silhouetting her father's rangy frame in the entrance. "Are you all right?"

"Sure, just great," she murmured.

Louis paused to snap on the overhead light, and the tulip-shaded fixture cast a soft glow on the rose-and-beige room. Sean blinked, then focused on her father. His thick gray hair was mussed around his almost gaunt face, and the deep red of the robe he wore over his gray pajamas made him look pale. She hadn't noticed the slight droop to his shoulders before, and for a moment she was struck by the fact that Louis was getting older.

He'd be sixty-five in a few months, but he was still strong, and she'd never thought of him as old. Until this moment, she hadn't noticed how deep the lines in his face were, bracketing at his mouth and fanning at the corners of his eyes. Or the way his gray hair now held just a hint of its original brown.

For as long as she could remember, it had been just her father and the business in her life. Somehow she had never thought about either one of them failing or not being there for her eventually. Now she was struck by the thought that both of them were vulnerable.

She swallowed hard. "What are you doing up at—" she glanced at the bedside clock, then sat forward and hugged her bent knees with her arms "—four in the morning?"

He shrugged as he came toward the bed. "I was awake thinking about things, and I heard you call out." He looked down at her from the side of the bed. "What's wrong?"

She shrugged, surprised that she'd made any sound Louis could have heard in his room. "I must have been dreaming." The rain beat on the windows with a vengeance, and she shivered involuntarily. "I guess it's the storm."

Louis sat on the side of the bed and looked right at her. His eyes were the same shade of amber as hers. "It's not the storm. It's the business."

"I guess so. I had no idea what I was walking into when you asked me to meet with Quint."

"I didn't, either. Quint just told me there was an emergency."

She touched her tongue to her lips. "How could it happen, Louis? The company's always been well run, never a doubt about its financial integrity. That's what makes us so strong, even in the recession."

"I wish I had the answers, but I don't."

"What if the answers damage us, and Warren International gets burned?"

"We'll deal with it if it comes to that."

"Louis, the money's gone. My God, it's enough to seriously damage the company."

He touched her arm, his fingers cool on her skin. "Sean, the company *will* survive. But I'm not so sure about you."

She could see the hint of teasing in his eyes, and she felt confused. The company had been everything for her father since her mother's death twenty-five years before, and it had meant everything to her for most of her twenty-eight years. It was the core of her father's life, and hers. "I hardly think this is funny, Louis."

He drew back. "I know it's not." His face sobered. "But I've been thinking a lot about it lately. That's why I was awake now."

"Of course, this trouble—"

"I wasn't thinking about the shortfall."

"Louis, I don't—"

He cut her off with a question that came so far out of left field that it made Sean blink. "I was wondering when you started calling me 'Louis' instead of 'Dad.'"

Nothing was the way it was supposed to be. "I don't remember." She shook her head, and her hair brushed against the bare skin of her shoulder. "Maybe it was when I started spending a lot of time at the office. Everyone called you Louis, so I did, I guess. Why?"

He stood abruptly and crossed to the windows, taking a while to look out at the stormy night before he spoke again. "We've never been the traditional family, have we?"

Sean stared at his back. "What's this all about?"

"I guess it's old age. I've been thinking about my own mortality. I was lying in bed thinking that I wouldn't mind having some part in the future."

She hated hearing him talk like that, and the thought of losing him made her chest tighten. He was the only person she loved. "Don't talk about this right now. Four in the morning, while it's storming, and while Warren's is in trouble, isn't the time to talk about . . . about that."

"That?" He turned, and when he spoke, his words made Sean's mouth drop open. "All right. Change of subject. You never said anything about this before, but I've been wondering if you ever considered having children."

A day of craziness had just gone off on another tangent that left her almost giddy with shock. "Children?"

"Grandchildren, for me. Those little human beings who keep going when you're gone, who give you that link with immortality, a piece of yourself living after you've gone."

She didn't know what to say. Children had never entered her mind, not even in the first few months of her marriage to Charles. She'd never pictured herself as a mother, and she'd certainly never pictured Charles as a father. "I can honestly tell you I haven't thought about it." She pinched the bridge of her nose between her thumb and forefinger and exhaled. "I didn't know that you'd ever thought about it, either."

"Actually, I hadn't, until recently. I never really talked to you or to Charles about it."

She laughed. The sound was cutting and dry. "For heaven's sake don't mention it to Charles when he comes back."

"When's he due?"

"I don't know. Maybe next week or the week after. He doesn't keep me informed unless he needs something from me."

"It sounds as if things aren't any better between the two of you."

She looked at him. "Louis, they aren't any better or any worse. They're under control. I made a mistake, but I can live with it."

"So dispassionate," he murmured.

"Sensible. I married the boy genius of the company, because I thought I loved him, because I thought I could trust him. I don't and I can't. I didn't know that he was so egocentric and self-indulgent. Now that I know, I can deal with it."

Her father stayed where he was, his back to the storm. "When I got married to your mother, there was passion and love and caring."

Another change of direction that surprised her. He never talked about her mother, yet she'd always known their relationship had been different. She hadn't gone into her own marriage, four years ago, with stars in her eyes. She'd admired Charles, in a lot of ways, and she'd thought she loved him. She'd thought he was a real asset to Warren International, and she'd thought they could make a marriage work. After his first "diversion" with a secretary, however, she'd lost any illusions about what they could have.

"Maybe you had that once with my mother, but what I remember is you working eighteen-hour days for years. You lived and breathed the company. I always thought you were the last true realist in this world."

He shook his head. "That only happens when there's little else in your life. With your mother gone, work seemed like the logical replacement. And I'll be damned, but I think I made you in my image."

"Would that be so bad? You taught me to see things in black and white, to make decisions with my head and not my emotions. Some decisions are good, some aren't."

"It's not a matter of good or bad—"

"Louis, you did what you had to do. That's what I do. I married Charles, and I shouldn't have. I foolishly let him get a large block of stock that would be invaluable in the hands of the wrong person bent on a takeover. I shouldn't have let that happen. His name's on the deed for the house on the island. It shouldn't be. But it is. So, I'm stuck with my mistake."

"Divorce the man and get it over with," Louis said.

"He doesn't want a divorce. He's told me if I press for one, he'll sell his stock to the highest bidder... as long as that bidder isn't you or me. And you know those stocks would be invaluable if there was a hostile takeover in the works."

"I know. But maybe we can get around it."

"Maybe. If you come up with an idea, let me know. Until then, Charles will use this marriage as his talisman against any of his 'friends' getting too close for comfort. As long as he stays in Europe most of the time and I stay here, it works out. He can lead his life any way he wants to, as long as he's discreet.''

Her father came back to stand by the bed. ''And what if you want to marry again?''

''That's not likely. Things are fine the way they are. What isn't fine is this trouble with the funds at the company.''

Louis pushed his hands into the pockets of his robe. ''After the Fourth, we find out what's going on.''

''I wish I hadn't planned the party on the island for the Fourth. This is no time to party and have fun, not when everything's falling apart. Maybe it'll keep raining and we can cancel.''

''Maybe the rain will go away and there'll be sun and you'll have your party.'' He yawned, then said, ''Whatever happens with everything, I'm going back to bed.''

''I'll see you before I leave tomorrow.''

''You'll go home and be on the computer all day, won't you?''

''Probably. Helen's taking care of all the party arrangements. I'll have the day free to see what I can find out.''

''For now, get some sleep.'' He turned and headed for the door. ''Good night, sweetheart.''

''Louis?''

He paused, his hand on the light switch. ''Yes?''

''Have you really been thinking about grandchildren?''

He lifted one brow. ''Just an old man's musings in the middle of the night.'' He snapped off the light, and the hall lights glowed at his back. ''Forget I even mentioned it.''

''Sure,'' she said as he left and closed the door behind him.

Sean sat in the dark, staring at the closed door, as she heard her father's footsteps in the hallway die out. Then she heard his bedroom door click shut. Slowly she slid down into the bed and tugged the sheets over her.

When she closed her eyes, she was struck once again by Louis's question about children. She'd never been a woman who was drawn to babies or thought she wouldn't be complete without a child. But as the storm raged outside, she suddenly thought about a child, her child.

Rolling onto her side, she pulled her knees up to her stomach and exhaled. Nonsense. There was no way she'd ever let Charles touch her again, and even though Charles had his affairs, she didn't have any desire to have one on her own.

She didn't need children. She had the business. She had her father. She had a life that she enjoyed on a lot of levels. She pushed the thoughts of children out of her mind, but as she drifted back to sleep, she felt a twinge of regret that the house she loved on Sanctuary Island would never be home to a child of her own.

A SUDDEN LOUD NOISE jolted Mac awake, and produced as much pain as a direct blow to his head would have. A scream stopped dead in his throat as he woke from a sleep so deep and black that he thought he must have passed out. It took a minute for him to realize the noise was outside of him, and the echoing was producing pain in his head, around his temples and behind his closed eyes.

As the sound went on and on, he eased his eyes open to a gray light that made his eyes ache, and he squinted to minimize the effect. He was in a car, leaning back against the seat, and through the front window he could see a mist, hiding everything more than ten feet ahead. A black Jeep was parked in front of him, and there was a huge shape beyond it, squat and blurred.

For a wrenching second he was lost, had no idea how or why he'd gotten here. Then he remembered the storm, the bar, drinking, and the accident. As he eased himself upward in the seat, he gingerly fingered the bandage at the pain center in his temple. The accident. Elliot. Dead. He squinted at the world outside. The storm had gone, leaving behind a misty fogginess.

When the sharp sound jarred him again, he turned to his left, the action protested by the ache in his head. Then sickness rose bitterly in his throat when he saw the torso of a man in a blue uniform with a badge on the left breast and a holster at the waist that held what looked like a 9 mm pistol.

God, it was over. Everything. They'd found him.

He swallowed as thoughts of things to do flashed through his mind, from swinging the door open into the cop's middle and taking off, to ramming the car he saw in the rearview mirror and forcing his way back up the ramp. But he didn't move. Whatever the bump had done to his head, it had taken its toll. And he was so weary of all the running.

When he reached for the power buttons on the door, he felt the coldness of metal, then pressed, and the window slid silently down. The air that drifted into the car was surprisingly warm, but damp and touched with the bite of the ocean. He gripped the steering wheel with his right hand and made himself look right at the cop as the man gripped the window frame and looked down into the car.

"It's almost time for the ferry, sir." Mac met the gaze of dark eyes under the brim of the uniform cap, and then he saw the patch on the cap. Sullivan Security Services. A rent-a-cop. The middle-aged guard was staring at Mac, making his neck tense and increasing the pounding in his head.

Then, unexpectedly, the man actually smiled at him. "Oh, Mr. Elliot, it's you. Didn't realize it. I haven't seen you for so long, and I didn't know you were back. Besides, I'm used to seeing you in that sports car."

All the crazy plans of the night before came back to Mac, the blurred reasoning that had made him think he could pass for Charles Elliot. Insanity. But now, when he was in this car, in these clothes, this man thought he was Charles Elliot. "Sports car?" he managed, his mouth dry and cottony.

"The red Porsche." The man's eyes narrowed again. "Say, what happened to your head?"

Mac touched the bandage again. The ache mingled with the throbbing of a mild hangover. The gauze felt rough against his fingertips, and he remembered the frozen moments when the car had come at him. "I had an accident." He swallowed to counter the dryness in his mouth.

"No wonder you can't remember the car."

"I'm a bit foggy," he murmured. It was a partial truth.

"Too bad the missus won't be there to greet you."

Mac didn't know if he'd heard the man right. "The missus?"

"Pretty blond lady?" the man asked with a grin.

Mac tried to smile, but it actually hurt to flex his facial muscles. "What . . . what about her?"

"You know, with me working here all the time, I can pretty much tell you who's on the island and who isn't. Your wife left yesterday morning and hasn't come back. You know how she is about her schedule. Well, she never came back last night. Friday nights she's pretty regular about coming back on the last ferry."

It struck Mac as odd that Charles Elliot's wife wasn't waiting for him. There was so much he didn't know. One thing helped, though—if Sean wasn't there right now, it took a load off him for a while. "I guess she got tied up with the business."

"I guess so." The man stood back. "Good to see you back, sir," he said. "The ferry's about ready for the first run. Now, I've got others to wake up."

Mac glanced at the name tag above the security badge. "Thanks, Marvin. I didn't intend to fall asleep."

"With that knock on the head, it's a good thing you didn't pass out. Hell, it's good you remember your own name."

The man's words struck Mac. If he couldn't remember a few things, if his thoughts were muddled from the blow to the head, it could cover up a lot of things he wouldn't know about Elliot's life. "I remember my name," he said, able to manage a faint smile.

"Good for you, Mr. Elliot," the man said with a smile, then moved back to the cars that were parked behind Mac.

Mac sank back in the seat and allowed himself a deep, rough exhalation. It was crazy, he thought, swallowing hard. But for now, at least, he was secure.

Mac looked ahead and saw that the fog had lifted a bit, exposing the ferry at the end of the angled ramp. It was large and bulky, anchored in a channel formed from scarred pilings, and it was painted a faded blue, with red strips around both upper and lower decks. The lower deck was for cars, and looked as if could take about twenty of them in two lanes that were separated by a cabin that ran down the middle of the wooden deck. The top deck looked as if it were for spectators.

Marvin walked back, nodded to Mac, and kept going past the Jeep to undo the massive chain that blocked the way to the ramp leading to the ferry's lower deck.

Mac turned on the car, then ran a hand over his face. The feeling of clean-shaven skin was strange to him, after having shaved only sporadically for the past four or five years. He glanced in the rearview mirror. The bandage on his left temple was a stark white, and his blue eyes were less than sharp.

"Charles Elliot," he murmured in the confines of the car. "Charles. Chuck? Charlie? Chuckie?" He stared into his own eyes. "Charles Elliot."

The sound of a fog horn vibrated through the air, and the Jeep started to inch forward. Mac slipped his car into gear and followed it down the ramp and onto the deck of the ferry. The Jeep was waved to the right, and when Mac was motioned to the left, he drove across the deck to the front of the ferry, where a safety chain blocked his way. A kid straddling the front rail gestured to him to stop.

Mac turned off the car and stared into the distance, into mist and fog and gray water that was choppy enough to make the ferry rise and fall. He glanced behind him as cars filed on, and then he felt the motors of the ferry start up, vibrating through the car. He couldn't see where they were going because of the heavy mists, but as the ferry moved down the channel to the open water, Mac knew he was finally going toward something, instead of away from everything.

SANCTUARY ISLAND came out of the mists after a ten-minute ferry ride, and Mac's first glimpse was of towering greenness, of land spreading out both north and south, with high bluffs fringed with massive trees. As the ferry slowed and eased into another channel made of pilings, then reversed its engines to stop, Mac closed his eyes. His headache had settled into a constant throbbing, and his eyes were aching.

A skinny teenager hurried past Mac's car and to the heavy chain. In a few seconds, the chain was to one side and the kid was motioning Mac off the ferry. He started the car and inched onto the inclined ramp and drove up into a parking area covered in heavy gravel. Four cars were in line for the trip back to Seattle.

Mac drove past the cars, the gravel crunching under his tires, and went toward a narrow two-lane road. He knew he had to go north, and he swung right onto the road. The blacktopped road climbed upward, cutting through the bluffs. Then, after a curve, it leveled out, snaking north through heavy growths of firs and massive broad-leaved trees.

Glimpses of the Sound to the right were stunning, with the rising July sun beginning to burn off the mists that haloed the water and the land.

The road cut inland, where it was canopied by trees and framed by low-growing ferns. Rain glistened on leaves, and Mac had to slow for puddles that still spotted the pavement. After less than a thousand feet, Mac spotted a carved wooden sign reading Look Out Point. He turned just beyond the sign onto gravel, and realized that it didn't go anywhere. It stopped not more than a hundred feet ahead at an impressive entry framed by twelve-foot-high stone pillars that supported wrought-iron gates. The number *10* was inset in the middle of both sides of the gates.

He stopped and stared at the heavy gates. Thinking was making his stomach ache and churn, and when he saw the call box to his left and no way to open the gates, sickness settled in his stomach like lead. He hadn't even thought about not being able to get onto the property.

He rolled down the window, breathed in fresh, warming air touched by the fragrance of flowers that couldn't be seen, by the ocean, and by the lingering rain. Then he pushed the button on the call box and heard a faint beeping, then ringing. But no one came on the line. Mac sat back and tried to think. There was no keypad, so no secret code. They had to get in *somehow*.

Then he remembered the key chain. He touched the small black rectangle hanging on the chain and saw that it had a single button on it. He pressed it. There was a hum, a click, and the gates swung slowly back.

Relieved, Mac drove onto a driveway of cobbled bricks that wound through a sea of emerald grass rimmed by towering pines far off to the left and right. The drive crested a low hill, then split, with one section going left and one right. As Mac took the right, he realized the drive was a circle that swung up to the front of the house.

It was strange that Mac hadn't even thought about what *home* would look like. Yet when he got his first glimpse of the house, it looked as if it belonged right where it was. The building was two stories, built of quarry rock and rough timber, with a moss-touched wooden shingle roof that had several stone chimneys rising from it.

"Home," Mac murmured, the word barely audible in the car. There hadn't been a home in his life for so long, he doubted he could even have imagined one.

He drove toward a portico that extended out of the second level to give protection to the main entrance. Supported by stone pillars, it stretched all the way across the cobbled parking area. He drove under it and stopped, then sat in the car and looked around at the arched windows set into the stone walls of the lower level, and at the ivy that wound around the posts of the portico. Clay pots of daisies framed the stone steps that led up to the entry doors, their bright yellow a splash of color against the brown and gray of the house.

He reached for the overnight bag, took the keys and got out. Circling the car, he went up the sweep of steps, sorted through the keys and put the most likely looking one in the lock. With that, Mac opened the door.

Chapter Three

Mac stepped into the total silence of a foyer that spanned the two stories, overlooked by a balcony at the top of a sweeping staircase to the right and filled with the scent of roses. As he stood on the highly polished parquet floor, he waited for a sound, or anything else to show there was someone here. But nothing moved.

"Hello?" he called, his voice echoing in the foyer.

Nothing. And Mac knew the house was empty. He could almost feel it. He was alone.

He pushed the door shut, and as a spell of dizziness hit him, the bag fell from his hand, and he reached to steady himself by pressing his hand flat against the wall. As he waited for the dizziness to settle, he closed his eyes, and inhaled deeply.

When he felt more settled, he opened his eyes again, and had a general impression of comfort and welcome. He saw a soft beige throw rug under his feet, then slowly looked up. The walls were done in a muted paisley paper, a blur of what he'd call forest colors, with touches of rose. The staircase was fashioned of dark, satiny-looking wood. The source of the rose fragrance, he saw, was an antique chest by the staircase that held a vase of deep red roses.

He glanced to his right at an arched doorway. Beyond that was a library with books from floor to ceiling, the pale morning light touching leather chairs and an impressive-looking chess set on a table in front of a series of windows. Off the foyer on the other side was what looked like a living room, with overstuffed sofas and chairs, and on the far wall a massive stone fireplace.

There was nothing really formal about this home; it was comfortable, almost gentle. A strange word to use, he thought, but he couldn't come up with another right now.

He stood without support, testing his balance, and exhaled as his head began to settle. He knew he should look around down here, that he should see where the hallway under the balcony led while no one was here, but he felt bone-weary, and the headache was making it hard to keep his eyes open.

Logically, the bedrooms should be upstairs. Leaving his case where it fell, he started for the staircase, but as he reached for the turned finial on the banister, he saw a note propped against the vase with the roses. He reached for the folded sheet of paper, opened it and read the precise script.

Helen: Check caterers. Make sure the tent is here early enough to be set up for the party. Also, check schedule for fireworks. Call office if there's a problem, and don't forget to hire locals for set up. Thanks. SWE.

Below the signature, someone had scrawled, "All under control. See you early Sunday morning. Helen."

He put the note back, shocked that his hand was trembling. God, he felt like he'd been run over by a bulldozer. He slowly started up the stairs, gripping the banister for support. Fireworks? Was it close to the Fourth of July now? He didn't have a clue. Days had come to run into weeks for him, with nothing to distinguish one from another. Until now.

There had been no big days in his life—at least no days he wanted to remember. He'd just survived, going from job to job. Making it on his own. His eyes blurred, and he paused to take a few deep breaths, then kept going. Charles Elliot had been building a life, while he had just lived his. But things were going to change. Everything was going to change. As soon as he was rested, as soon as his head stopped pounding and his eyes could focus, he'd face his new life.

SEAN SLOWED her Mercedes for a policeman directing traffic around a barricade on a side street near the docks. Glancing up the street as she passed it, she barely took in a group of people in front of a cheap bar, and cops measuring something on the road. Her mind was full of the meeting yesterday, and her last talk with her father.

As she gripped the steering wheel, she spotted the ferry landing ahead. Glancing at the clock in her Mercedes, she was surprised to see that it was barely noon. It felt as if she had been up for days. Her sleep the night before had been so restless, and after her father had left, her dreams had been unsettling.

A muddled maze of Quint telling her about the electronic transfers of massive amounts of company funds from different branches of Warren was mixed up with her father asking her about grandchildren. She swung toward the ferry and headed down the ramp, thankful that she had hit the time exactly. The ferry was ready to take off, and she was the last car eased onto the deck before the safety chain was put in place.

"Hello, there," someone called, and Sean turned to see one of the security guards at the ferry landing wave to her and smile. She thought his name was Marvin. He was a talker, and she didn't feel like that right now. So she returned the wave, then looked away and sank back in the seat of her car.

The motors of the ferry ground to life, and just knowing she was going home to the island helped to ease some of the knots in her stomach. Home. God, she loved that house. A wedding present from her father, it was the best thing he had ever given her. Ten acres, a view of the Sound, and a peace that was all hers while Charles was in Europe.

At least she had a week or so before he'd show up. She'd put up with his comings and goings for a couple of weeks, and then he'd be gone again. The house would be all hers for a while. She smiled at that thought. All hers.

That sense of growing peace lasted for Sean until she drove over the cobbles of the driveway and saw a strange car parked under the portico. When she spotted a rental-company sticker on the back bumper, she knew Charles was back. No call. No warning. She hated him for dropping into her world right now.

She parked her Mercedes behind the rental, grabbed her purse and hurried to the stairs. She went up to the doors, hoping against hope that Charles had just come back to get a few things, to leave the rental car to be picked up by the company, and then left again to go back to the city.

When she stepped into her home, she felt her confidence rise. There wasn't a sound in the stillness, and the scent of roses hung in the air. There wasn't a hint of the cigars that Charles had favored on his last trip back. He wasn't here. She crossed and picked up the note she'd left for Helen, read what the housekeeper had added to her original writing, then laid it facedown on the chest.

Helen would be here tomorrow—the party was tomorrow evening—but for now she was alone. She had the house all to herself. She'd change into comfortable clothes, then get on the computer in the office. As she climbed the stairs, her footsteps were muffled by the Persian runner, and she skimmed her fingertips over the satiny finish of the turned banister.

Perfect for sliding down. The thought came from nowhere, and it made her stop two stairs from the top. A memory from her childhood materialized, the house in the city, the banister, her sliding down it, flying off the end, crashing into an umbrella stand and getting four stitches in her upper lip.

She touched the small scar on her lip. A five-year-old had no idea of consequences. And when she'd split her lip and seen the blood, she'd been sure she was dying. "Banisters are made for sliding down," her father had assured her as he got ice and towels, "but only if you figure out how to stop *before* you start down." He'd carried her to the car to go to the doctor's office. "A life lesson, sweetheart" he'd said. "Always figure out how to stop before you start."

"Figure out how to stop," she whispered, looking back at the long length of stairs behind her. Since that day, she knew, she'd been figuring out how to stop before doing anything in her life. Only a few times she hadn't, and she'd paid for it. Charles was one of those slips, a blip in sanity because she'd thought she could love him and make a life with him.

She turned, went up onto the balcony, then turned right to head down the short hall to the double doors of the master bedroom suite that occupied the whole north wing. Now all she had to do was figure out how to stop whatever was happening to Warren International.

She pushed back the doors and stepped into the quiet coolness of the suite. In the broad hallway, which was lined by mirrored wardrobe doors on either side, she slipped off her dark pumps, then wiggled her toes in the off-white carpeting. Her purse slipped from her hand to settle by her shoes as she stretched her hands over her head to try to ease the tension that tugged at her shoulders and neck.

With a deep sigh, she freed her shoulder-length hair from the sliver clip that had held it in a low twist, then ran her fingers through the strands, combing them back from her face. She opened the sliding doors to the closet, barely looking at her reflection in the mirrors. She knew she looked tired, and she hadn't bothered with any makeup. There was an impression of paleness, of her white silk blouse and navy skirt, of her exhausted expression.

She stepped into the closet, dropped her shoes on a shelf to her left, then undid the pearl buttons on her blouse. She tugged it loose from the straight skirt, then shrugged out of it and put it on the table for dry cleaning. She unzipped her skirt, let it fall around her ankles, then stepped clear of it and put it with her blouse.

She took off her panty hose and tossed them on the other clothes, then found a pair of blue shorts and a T-shirt from the drawers at the back. She took the clothes and went back into the hall in her white bikini pants and white lace bra. She paused to pick up her purse, then padded into the bedroom to go across to the bath suite.

The room was in soft shadows, with just slivers of sunlight sneaking between the panels of the pale blue drapes pulled over the French doors that opened onto the balcony, which looked out over the Sound. Sean barely glanced at the room itself, at the massive armoire by the arched entry to the bath and sauna, the old-fashioned chaise covered in blue chintz near the view windows, the stone fireplace that occupied most of the side wall. And the king-size plantation bed stripped of its gauze canopy and curtains and covered with a peach-and-blue comforter, that stood facing the view.

As she headed past the bed, Sean was anxious to change and get to the computer in her home office. This business was so disturbing that it made her stomach ache. She tossed her purse to her right, aiming for the bed. Two million dollars, minimum. Damn it, she—

A vibrating curse cut through the stillness, and she froze. For a split second she thought she'd imagined the oath, or that she'd uttered it herself. Then it came again, and even though it echoed her own frustration, she knew she hadn't said it. And she knew that someone was in the room with her, someone with a deep, harsh voice that echoed in the stillness.

Slowly, she turned, her heart in her throat, and she watched in horror as someone reared up out of her bed, tossing the comforter to one side. As the cover slid onto the ivory carpet, Sean felt fear making her sick. When she could finally see the intruder, she realized he wasn't some demented burglar.

Charles sat in her bed, his image blurred by the low light. But she could see him, his hair mussed around his face, one hand bracing him in a sitting position, the other rubbing his shoulder. His eyes were narrowed on her.

"Damn it, Charles," she gasped, her hand pressed to her breast. "You scared me to death!"

He didn't give any indication that he heard what she said. He just sat in the tangled linen, watching her, a stark white gauze bandage at his temple. In the stillness, she could hear his breathing, and the quick, ragged sound grated on her nerves.

"Charles," she said, heading toward him, "get out of my bed."

She sidestepped his clothes, which were heaped in a pile by the bed. Her first instinct was to toss him out of the room—a silly idea, when you compared their sizes. But that didn't stop her from grabbing his forearm.

As her fingers closed around the sinewy arm, she heard him take a hissing breath, and she felt him tense, his muscles hard under her touch. Then he slowly looked down at her hand on him. Her skin was surprisingly pale against his. For a heartbeat, she was certain he was either going to grab her hand and yank it off him or pull her into the bed with him. That last thought made her wish she'd never touched him.

When he finally looked up to meet her gaze, she barely fought back an involuntary gasp. For what seemed an eternity, she was faced with a gaze so intense and so disturbing that breathing became impossible for her.

Charles was impossible. Charles was irritating. Charles was selfish. But Charles had never been a man who could look at her and take away her ability to move or do anything rational. Not Charles. Not ever. Yet now, with her touching him, she found the world narrowing precariously to nothing but senses and feelings.

She snatched her hand back as if she had touched fire, and pushed them behind her back. Her nerves were raw from the problems with the business. That was what this was all about. And here was Charles sitting in her bed, and she was overreacting in the most ludicrous way.

"All right. Enough," she muttered, fighting the urge to rub away the lingering feeling of his skin against hers. But she settled for curling the hand into a fist behind her back and digging her nails into her palms. "Get out."

He finally spoke, in a low, hoarse voice. "Sean?"

"Whose bedroom did you think you were in?" she asked, shocked by the bitterness that tinged her question. Hadn't she been the one to tell Charles to do as he wished, just as long as he didn't embarrass her or the business?

He finally looked away and moved, but she wasn't so sure that was what she wanted after all. The idea that he might be naked under the linen barely formed before the sheets were gone. Relief felt heady when Sean saw that he was wearing white boxer shorts.

She moved back abruptly as he slowly swung his legs over the side of the bed, then sat there, his head in his hands, as he took several deep breaths. He exhaled harshly, then lifted his head and looked up at her again. As their eyes met, she became horribly aware that she was almost as naked as he was.

Where had this embarrassment come from? She felt shaky and off center, but there was no way she was going to try to cover herself right now. Silently she watched as he levered himself to a standing position and grabbed the post at the foot of the bed.

He looked unsteady on his feet, and she had an idea. "Are you drunk?"

His tongue touched his lips, and when he coughed softly, he flinched. "Had a bit, but . . ." His voice was still hoarse, edged with a roughness that made it seem deeper.

He was hung over, and he'd found his way into her bed. "I guess you did," she said, but she wasn't really thinking about his drinking habits. As he stood unsteadily not more than four feet from her, she wondered when Charles had lost weight, and when he'd let his hair grow longer. He had been peripheral to her life for so long that she didn't even remember when she'd really looked at him last. And certainly she couldn't remember when she'd looked at him and had her heart lurch or her mouth go dry. God, she felt like some teenager, staring at him in his underwear. But she was unable to look away.

"I...I hit my head, and I..." He touched the bandage at his temple with the tips of his fingers. "I'm a bit foggy."

She looked at the scrape under the bottom of the bandage and frowned. Sean hadn't felt anything for Charles for so long, it took her a minute to realize she felt sympathy for him, along with other things. Other things? She almost laughed at that lame euphemism. She couldn't remember ever seeing Charles look so damned sexy, drunk or sober.

How in heaven's name could this man go off to Paris for nine months and come back as a man who stood in front of her nearly naked, making her think things that she honestly couldn't remember ever having thought before?

"The doctor said it...it's a slight concussion. He said there might be side effects."

She made herself ask, "Like what?"

"Dizziness, sickness...memory lapses."

She laughed at that. It was a bitter, humorless sound that faltered as soon as it began. The white cotton shorts, incredibly stark against his tanned skin, showed that the former softness of his build was definitely gone. Now there were hard muscles, lean hips, a flat stomach, and—

"What's so funny?" he asked.

She caught herself before she started down a figurative banister without any idea of how to stop at the end. And she had to stop this . . . now. Charles wasn't sexy, and he certainly wasn't desirable, she told herself. She could turn away from him and leave without regretting it. "Only a memory lapse would make you think you were welcome in here."

Mac didn't have any memory of coming into this room, or undressing or getting into this bed. The last thing he remembered was coming into the house, standing in a foyer, and his head pounding as if it had been hit by a train. The next thing he knew, something had torn him out of nightmares that had gone in vicious circles. He felt a nagging ache in his shoulder, and knew he'd been hit by something. He eased his glance to the bed and saw a black handbag lying in the tumble of sheets.

He slowly looked back at the woman not more than three feet from him, her image blurred by eyes that refused to focus clearly. In some scrambled thought process during the night, he'd thought about the moment when he'd come face-to-face with Sean Warren-Elliot. He'd thought about convincing her he was Charles Elliot, but she'd know he wasn't her husband, she'd scream, call the cops, and he'd be back where he began, in New Orleans and locked up.

But this woman was buying the charade that he was her husband. And even with his blurred vision, she was stunning. The picture in the wallet hadn't come close to the reality. Nothing had prepared him for her sleek sexiness, for high breasts restrained by a flimsy, lacy excuse for a bra, a flat stomach, the swell of hips, and slender legs that seemed to go on forever. And absolutely nothing had prepared him for her touch.

Making contact with other people wasn't his strong suit. He'd avoided it most of his life, but when she'd caught him by the arm, he'd felt a jolt as volatile as lightning cut through him. He hadn't moved, because he'd been unable to, and when he'd looked in her eyes, he'd thought he saw the same reaction there, an echo of a need that could have flared into an inferno.

But that didn't add up with the angry words and the edge in her husky voice. She and her husband had a problem, and Mac didn't have any idea what that problem was. Maybe there'd been a fight, a misunderstanding. Maybe that was the reason Elliot had been in Europe for nine months, not just company business. But one thing he knew for sure—she was clearly accepting him as Charles Elliot.

She took a step toward him, bringing a hint of a fragrance that seemed a mingling of flowers and freshness. "Didn't you hear what I said, Charles?" she asked, studying him closely.

He looked down into her eyes. Even though the pain in his head was making his stomach churn, he was almost thankful for it. The diversion of pain kept him from a reaction that would be more than evident in his nearly naked state. He narrowed his eyes to dull her image, but it backfired on him. It actually helped him focus better.

"I can tell when I'm not wanted," he managed around the dryness in his mouth.

"Good," she said, crossing her arms.

"Just point me to aspirins and a place to sleep."

"You know where to sleep, but I can manage a couple of aspirins," she muttered, walking toward what he assumed was the bathroom.

He slowly turned, still holding on to the bedpost, and watched her cross the room and go through a wide archway. Lights flashed on, and the brilliance made his head contract horribly. He looked away, but not before he saw a space lined with vanities on both sides, and what looked like a massive sunken tub straight ahead.

After a few moments, the lights flashed off and he turned to see Sean coming back. She'd put on a white terry-cloth robe cinched at her slender waist, and she had a glass of water in one hand. When she got back to where he stood, she held out the glass in one hand and a small plastic bottle in the other. "Aspirin and water."

He took the glass and sipped some of the cool liquid, letting it ease the dryness in his mouth and throat. Then he slowly let go of the bedpost and held out his other hand, palm up. "Would you hand me four aspirin, please?"

She hesitated, then twisted off the top and shook four pills out onto his palm. Mac tossed the pills into his mouth, washed them down with water, then handed the glass back to Sean. "Thanks."

"Didn't the doctor give you anything?"

"He just said aspirin and rest." He exhaled and asked, "Where do I sleep?"

His vision was getting clearer all the time, and he could see that she was looking at him as if he were joking. Then he saw the way the fullness of her pale lips tightened. "In *your* room."

So this wasn't a passing argument. He had his own room. "Just where is . . . *my* room?"

"For heaven's sake, Charles, I—"

"Humor me. Tell me where my room is."

She hesitated, then motioned with the hand that held the bottle of aspirin. "Out the door, across the balcony." Before he could ask anything else, she added, "The second door on the right." She moved around him, scooped up his clothes and shoes, then held them out to him. "And take these with you."

He took the bundle from her, then slowly turned and looked for the exit. When he spotted what he thought would be the way out, past mirrored doors, he started for it.

"Charles?"

He paused, certain he was heading for a closet instead of the door to the hallway. He glanced back, careful not to jar his head, and saw Sean by the bed, holding on to the post that had helped support him. "What?"

"Is the rental company coming for the car?"

He closed his eyes for a moment, then said, "I didn't even think about it."

"I'll call them."

"Thanks." He turned away from her, and only took a single step before she spoke up again.

"Charles?"

He stopped without turning, not wanting to see her again, standing there in the soft light, looking for all the world like a vision he might have had in his imagination. "What?"

"When are you leaving?"

He stared at the closed door ahead of him. "I don't know."

"You never stay longer than two weeks."

"I'll be here for a while, at least," he said, hedging.

"Why did you come back early?"

He closed his eyes. "Why wouldn't I?"

"Why would you?" she countered.

He didn't know what to say, and his ability to think was rapidly escaping him. "I don't know," he murmured, and went to the door. He opened it, then stepped out into the hall and closed the door behind him. With soft carpet under his feet, he stood still for a moment.

Why had Charles come back? He couldn't remember what the man had said, something about being back and ready to set things right. Maybe he'd meant the marriage. And why did Sean want him gone so badly?

He went out on the balcony and to the second door on the right. He opened the door on a smaller room with dark furniture, beige carpet and drapes across the entire back wall that blocked the sunlight. The room was in good taste, yet it looked as impersonal as a hotel room. Charles Elliot obviously hadn't considered this home at all.

He felt as if he'd stepped into an unsolvable riddle. Mac dropped his clothes on a chair by the door, then crossed to the king-size bed. Everyone had such huge beds in this house. He tugged back the beige spread and slipped in between the cool white sheets. As he thought about Sean, and the fact that she seemed to hate her husband, the aspirin began to work. The pain in his head had eased, and he let himself go into welcome sleep.

SEAN WATCHED the door close behind Charles, and then she slowly turned and sank down on the bed. Her world felt upside down, and having Charles here was the topper. No, the topper was her reaction to him. "Stupid," she muttered, then stood. "Really stupid." Maybe it came from her father's crazy remarks about grandchildren.

One thing she knew. It didn't matter if Charles was here or not. He'd leave soon enough. Either he'd go into the city to play with a "friend," or he'd get bored quickly and head back to Paris. Either way, she wouldn't let him further complicate her life.

She went into the bathroom and turned on the sauna by the tub. She set the temperature, then slipped out of her clothes and wrapped her hair in a towel, turban-style. Then she stepped into the dry heat of the wooden-walled sauna. She inhaled the air, then sank down on one of the benches that ran along the wall.

As she sat back and closed her eyes, the image of Charles by the bed materialized. The skimpy briefs, the dark skin and hard stomach. She opened her eyes quickly and stared at the wooden wall. She'd been celibate for almost four years, but she'd never thought much about it. Sex with Charles had been passable at best, and she actually couldn't remember it very well.

But with that image in her mind of Charles by the bed, she wondered if she'd given up too easily. Maybe she should have tried harder to make a marriage out of their arrangement. Then she thought about the other women who had been in his life since then. No, there was no marriage.

MAC COULDN'T REMEMBER dreaming much in his life, and when he had, they had been nightmares. He was having nightmares again. Since the accident, every time he closed his eyes, incoherent visions overwhelmed him, a horrible hodgepodge of losing control, striking pavement, and seeing a man dead on the road with his face torn.

But in this nightmares, *he* was on the pavement, Mac Gerard, dead, with nothing. The rain soaking him. The sirens and the police. And Charles Elliot taking off in the car and disappearing into the night. These were the nightmares he remembered.

But now, there were also dreams. In them, he felt a soft peacefulness everywhere, with gentle sounds he couldn't recognize, and a soft darkness that seemed to wrap around him like velvet. He settled into it, and then the voice came, a soft, husky voice that seemed to echo deep in his soul.

The words were unintelligible, but their effect on him was crystal-clear. Mac felt a sense of belonging that he'd never known in his life. He felt centered and grounded, and the feelings were so intense that he could feel his chest tighten.

Then the shadows moved, and he could see someone coming to him out of the darkness, closer and closer. With agonizing slowness, the image began to define, and finally he could see Sean coming to him. Strangely, he had known it was her from the start. Her hair was loose, a pale veil around her almost ethereal face. Shadowed eyes, full lips, her chin tilted just a bit, her neck a graceful sweep, ears small and delicate.

And she was talking, murmuring things that ran across his nerves, making every atom of his being respond. That response intensified when he realized she was wearing a wisp of gauze, a mere suggestion of a covering that in no way hid her body. He knew he groaned, he could feel the vibration run through him, yet in the dream the only sounds were her soft whisperings.

She came closer, closer, her body defined with a clarity that took his breath away. And she was holding out her arms to him, welcoming him. But he couldn't move. He couldn't make himself reach out to her. Yet all he wanted was to touch her, to pull her to him, to know her and explore her. All he wanted was to be with her and block out the world. And he knew he'd find true sanctuary in her arms.

Chapter Four

Mac could finally move in the dream, and he reached out for Sean, intending to touch her, hold her, know her. But as he raised his hands toward her, she smiled at him, her eyes warmed by the glow of need, and he heard a single clear word. "Charles."

His hands closed on nothing but air, and an ache hit him in the middle. He could feel the heat fleeing, to be replaced by a chill that made him tremble, and no matter how hard he tried to reach her, she was out of his reach and fading into little more than a wraith.

He knew her presence was leaving him as surely as that feeling of belonging was, as if it had never been. The cold skimmed over him, around him, through him, and he went from sleep to wakefulness in the time it took for his heart to beat once.

He lay in the large bed. The room was deep in shadows. He was alone. As alone as he'd been all his life. But in that moment when the dream had vanished, he'd felt a true loneliness deep in him that he couldn't remember feeling before. Realistically, he knew it had little to do with real life, and everything to do with his dream of Sean Elliot. But it ached nonetheless.

He lay very still, absorbing the feelings, and then he realized that the pain was physical too. The ache behind his eyes was less intense, and his neck was tight. The pain came from elsewhere. He didn't have to look to see what the dream's effects had been on him. It seemed incredible that a woman in a dream had affected him more than a lot of flesh-and-blood women had in his life. That thought actually made him smile wryly.

Women. There'd been women, all right, especially when he'd been younger. But he couldn't remember any one woman in particular. Their faces blurred and ran together. No one important. No one he'd stayed with longer than he felt like staying. He hadn't allowed them to be part of him, or part of his life.

He stretched carefully, then turned his head from side to side and saw the lit face of the clock by the bed. Ten o'clock. But he had no idea if it was in the morning or night, if he'd slept hours or even days. The dream could have lasted a few moments or an eternity.

Tossing the sheets off, he levered himself to the side of the bed and sat there for a moment, listening. He couldn't hear any sounds at all. Slowly he stood up, and he found the discomfort bearable. He touched his shoulder and flexed it. All in all, he wasn't too bad.

He slowly walked to the wall of curtains and tugged one side away from a large picture window. It was night, with a full moon suspended in a dark sky, its light reflecting back off the black waters of the Sound, below the high bluffs the house was built on. Far off he could see a halo of lights in the night, probably from the skyline of Seattle. It looked so far away, as if it were another world.

Another world. What he wanted was another life, and what had begun on impulse, and with the help of being a bit drunk, was solidifying. Charles Elliot's wife thought he was her husband. That couldn't have been a dream. Not like the last part of his memory. No, Sean Elliot had looked at him with anger, with frustration, but without any doubt about who he was.

And with their marriage difficulties, it worked better. It gave him a cushion of space. He wouldn't be expected to be the loving husband, at least not for a while. A loving husband to Sean? The idea tightened his body instantly, and he pushed it away, refusing to think about the dream again.

He turned to the room, which was bathed in moonlight. For now he'd sleep here. He'd find out sooner or later why Charles had set up his quarters in here, instead of the master bedroom. But for now it would work for him. At least he had a place where he didn't have to watch his every step, where he didn't have to watch what he said and what he did, until he knew what was expected of him.

For now, he had to look around the house and get his bearings. Since it was night, this was his chance to look around without anyone seeing him. He went to the bed and snapped on a lamp. He was about to cross to the sliding doors by the open bathroom door, but he stopped when he saw a television set in an arched alcove opposite the bed.

He crossed the room and turned it on, flipping the stations until he found a news program with a weather map filling the screen. "...and the storm that drenched the city has passed to the west, to take its moisture inland, and Seattle looks forward to a bright, sunny July fourth," a voice-over said. "Tonight's low will be a moderate sixty degrees, and for tomorrow's high we'll be looking at a pleasant seventy-eight."

The picture shifted to a silver-haired man in a red blazer, backed by a picture of the skyline of Seattle. "And in another storm-related item, a man was killed at two o'clock this morning when he was struck by a hit-and-run driver outside the Belly Up Bar and Grill, near the docks. The victim, tentatively identified as Mackenzie Gerard from New Jersey, was pronounced dead at the scene from massive internal injuries and head trauma.

"A man who left the bar with Gerard is being sought by police for questioning. If anyone has information about this case, please contact the Seattle Police Department. In other news, the dam at—"

Mac snapped off the television and stared at the empty screen. He was dead. Mackenzie Gerard had been killed on a Seattle street in the middle of a storm. He closed his eyes for a long moment, then exhaled in a rush. Charles Elliot was home. He went into his bathroom and turned on the shower.

Stripping naked, he got under the warm water and let it wash over him. Charles Elliot had a life. Charles Elliot had problems with his wife, but they could be worked out somehow. Charles Elliot was a very lucky man.

Mac realized that the life of Mackenzie Gerard had ended as anonymously as it had been lived—until New Orleans. He lifted his face into the stream of water, and for an unsettling moment his life passed through his mind. He'd heard that happened to people just before they died. Maybe that was why it was happening to him now.

Mac had flashing memories of the foster homes, some decent, some little more than holding centers. And the old suitcase he had had since the first, a battered container that had held everything he had in the world. The moment he'd taken off, when he'd decided that living on the streets was preferable to being pushed into another slot.

The jobs, everything from ditch digging to computers to the docks. People who'd wandered in and out, no friends, just acquaintances, and women who'd been there, and then gone. Then the final escape. Walking away from the jail, from New Orleans, then landing in Seattle on a rainy night that changed everything.

Mac stayed under the water, trying to absorb the finality of what he'd done. Mackenzie Gerard's life was over. And he was going to grab Charles Elliot's life with both hands. He turned off the water, then stepped out into the bathroom, a man who had become real in the past few minutes. Grabbing a towel, he began to dry off. It was time to get squared away. First he'd look through the house, get his bearings, and then he'd go over the papers in the briefcase.

After he put a fresh bandage on the abrasion on his forehead, he went into the bedroom, slid back the doors of the walk-in closet and found racks of neatly ordered clothes covered with plastic drop cloths. He tugged back part of the covering and found shirts, slacks and jackets. On the right side, the plastic-covered shelves held sweaters, shoes, underwear and socks.

He grabbed a white short-sleeved shirt and a pair of jeans that still had the wrappings from a dry cleaners on them. He slipped on the clothes, leaving the shirt untucked, then went to the door barefoot. He stepped out into the darkened hall and went to the stairs. At the top of the stairs, he stopped to look at the closed doors to Sean's room beyond. No lights showed, so he started down the stairs to look around Charles Elliot's home.

SEAN HAD BEEN at the computer for so long, her neck and shoulders were beginning to knot. She'd tried to trace the path of money through the company, but she always ran into a brick wall. The money had disappeared as easily as water trickling through a sieve. It shocked her. The company was vulnerable in ways that she hadn't even considered before.

She hit the Enter button and sat back as the computer started its search for records on a business deal that had taken place six months before at their New York office. Just as the facts came up on the screen, Sean sensed that she wasn't alone, that she was being watched. Her finger hovered over the Enter button as she turned and looked behind her at the doorway to the cluttered room.

She'd known logically that it had to be Charles, but she still flinched inside when she saw him. What right did he have to look so casually sexy? She pulled her hand back and closed it into a fist, resting it in her lap. His dark hair looked as if he had carelessly combed it back from his face by running his fingers through it.

A beard was beginning to darken his jaw, and his eyes were clearer now, bluer, and even more intense in their scrutiny.

In an untucked white shirt that only emphasized his tanned skin, and jeans that looked indecent with the top button undone, the man was disturbing. It was as if Sean were looking at a stranger. That thought shocked her. Had she been so indifferent to Charles that the moment she noticed him it was as if she were meeting him for the first time? She shied away from that thought.

"What do you want?" she asked, her voice more clipped than she'd meant it to be.

He leaned one shoulder against the door frame and shrugged. The fine material of his shirt moved with his shoulders. "I didn't expect to find you here."

She almost asked where he'd expected to find her, but the memory of the encounter in her room was still too fresh for her to utter the question. "I'm working." She looked away from Charles and stared at the computer screen. "I thought you would be long gone by now."

"Where would I be long gone to?"

She stared at the images on the screen. They were beginning to blur. "How would I know?"

She knew he was moving, that he was coming closer, but she refused to look up at him. "If a wife doesn't know where—"

That did it. Sean got to her feet, almost bumping into Charles, who was right beside her chair now. She moved back to give herself some space, gripping the back of the leather chair she'd been sitting in. "That's it. I don't know what your game is this time, but you can forget about it."

He was motionless, gazing at her so intently that she felt heat rising in her face. Damn him. Suddenly he could make her feel embarrassed at being without makeup and in old shorts and a shapeless top. His blue eyes didn't blink, and his quiet scrutiny was more unnerving to her than if he'd screamed at her.

"Game?" he finally asked softly.

"Maybe I should have said *trouble*. What kind of trouble are you in now?" Right now she didn't have the emotional reserves to deal with any of this, but she needed to know. "What's happening that you came back a week early?"

"Couldn't I have just wanted to come home early?"

All Charles wanted at "home" was to know the current market value of the house or how high the stock had risen in the company. "Sure, and I bet you've got swampland for sale," she muttered.

He cocked his head to one side, and for a moment she could have sworn he was going to smile. A light touched his eyes, but it was gone so quickly, she wondered if she'd imagined it. "I don't have any swampland, and you talk in riddles," he said with studied soberness.

"Just what is it that you don't understand, Charles?" she asked, exasperated as much by her own strange reactions as by his barely hidden humor.

He didn't move. "I came home. You're acting as if that's a federal offense."

She turned from him and went to the windows behind the desk. The huge moon cast a silvery glow over the back area, and the waters in the distance. She loved this place, this house, this room, but she felt suffocated with Charles standing so close to her. "All right. I won't talk in riddles."

"Good. I'm terrible at deciphering them."

She kept her eyes on the night outside, even though she was totally aware of each breath Charles took, not more than two feet from her. "You only come back here for specific reasons. Being at home isn't one of them."

"What are my reasons, then?" he asked.

That was easy. "The best reason is to check in with head office. The worst reason is that you're in trouble. You need money. You got bored." She cast him a slanting glance, not knowing what she expected to see in his expression. But it wasn't dead seriousness as he considered each item she ticked off. "Or you decided to take my offer and came to get it over with in person."

"Riddles again?" he asked, one eyebrow lifted slightly.

"Charles," she said, exhaling in exasperation. "I—"

"Couldn't I just come home early?" he asked, his words touched with dogged reason.

She knew her expression tightened, and she wished she could bite out some cutting answer. But the words weren't there for her. She shrugged and looked away from him, making herself take a breath before saying, "No."

"This is my house, too, isn't it?" he asked.

Her hands tightened so much that her nails bit into her palms. "Of course it is. Both of our names are on the deed."

"That's usual for a husband and wife," he murmured.

Husband? The word sounded mocking to her. She'd never had a real husband. "Have you reconsidered my offer?"

"What offer are you talking about?"

She wished she could shake him or scream at him, but she found herself remaining motionless. "I want to buy your share of this house. There's no point in you holding on to it. You're here no more than two weeks out of any given year. You could get a hotel room that would do just as well for you, and you'd be in the city, instead of stuck out here on the island."

He exhaled, and she felt the heat of his breath brush her bare arm. Fighting the urge to rub her skin where the heat lingered, she waited for Charles to say something. But when he spoke, it shocked her. "Why would you want to buy my share of this place? Are you planning on a divorce?"

"That's it," she muttered, and tugged at the chair. She sat down and stared at the computer screen. "Just go away. I should have known you wouldn't do anything honestly and aboveboard."

She heard him move, but he didn't leave the room. Instead, she caught movement out of the corner of her eye, and glanced up to see Charles seating himself in the chair that faced her desk. "You really don't understand English, do you?" she said.

He settled back, lacing his fingers loosely on his middle and resting one bare foot on a denim-clad knee. "I understand English."

"Then the bump on your head did more damage than the doctors thought."

His eyes narrowed. "Why don't you tell me what's wrong?"

She sat back in her chair, barely able to meet his direct gaze. "What are you talking about?"

"There's obviously something wrong here." He motioned to indicate the computer. "It's almost midnight, and you're sitting in front of a computer, and you're tight as a coiled spring and so mad you could spit nails. No matter how you feel about me, I can't believe it's all because I came home early."

She wished she could say that was exactly what the problem was, but she couldn't lie about it. There had been enough lying between them. "It is . . . partly."

"Just partly? What's the other part?"

"The business."

"What's going on with the business?"

This was all wrong. Charles couldn't care less about the business, unless he thought he was going to lose money. His job at the Paris office was as little more than a figure head, with others doing the basic work. "Why do you care? Your stock is secure . . . for now."

"Why don't you just tell me what's going on, and I'll let you know if I care or not."

She exhaled, shocked that part of her wished she could really share this with Charles. But this marriage wasn't anything close to an Ozzie-and-Harriet scenario. It never had been. It never would be. And Charles was never there for her. Physically he might be in this room, looking for all the world as if he really wanted to know, but she wasn't foolish enough to believe it was true. "There's a bit of a crisis at the company, and I'm trying to figure it out."

When he stood and came around the desk to stand behind her, her instinct was to shut down the computer. But she didn't move as he bent down and scanned the screen over her shoulder. She could feel his heat at her back, and she found herself holding her breath. She didn't need to inhale the scent of maleness that clung to him.

As he moved to point at the screen, his arm brushed her shoulder, and she stiffened even more. "What are these figures?" he asked, his voice close to her left ear.

She could barely focus on the monitor. "Profit-and-loss figures for April and May for the New York office."

"How does it look?"

"Not really good." She closed her eyes. "I'm trying to figure out what happened."

He moved back, and for a heartbeat Sean was grateful that his closeness was erased. But the relief fled when he touched her shoulders, and she involuntarily jumped at the contact. "Hey, take it easy," he murmured, his fingers on her shoulders.

When she stilled, he began to knead her knotted muscles, the strength in his fingers digging at the tension, and she closed her eyes. She could barely cope with anything right now, let alone Charles trying to be—What? Human? A husband? She suddenly remembered her father talking about children, the crazy idea of grandchildren. What had seemed strange at the time took on a new meaning for her. Being touched by Charles was almost pleasurable, but she knew how dangerous it could be to trust anything Charles said or did.

"That...that's better," she managed as she moved forward and away from his touch. But it wasn't. As soon as he broke the contact, the tightness began to come back. Biting her lip, Sean saved her file and went out of the program to shut off the computer.

Mac knew he should back up and let the distance between Charles and his wife stay intact, but Sean made it impossible for him to do that. When he'd looked at her across the desk, he'd seen the worry in her expression. And something in him, a particle of empathy that he hadn't felt for a very long time, couldn't be denied.

When he'd touched her, kneading her shoulders, it had been all he could do to keep his touch therapeutic. He'd been looking down at her pale hair the way he was now, and he'd been overwhelmed by the urge to inhale its freshness. God, for a man who had never wanted to be "involved" on any level, he was feeling remarkably involved with a woman he barely knew.

"How much money are we talking about?" he asked, partially to tamp down feelings that he didn't know how to cope with.

She turned and looked up at him. Her eyes were shadowed by long lashes, but he could still see the concern there. "Too much."

Why should he suddenly feel protective of this woman? "How much?" he persisted, trying to block his thoughts.

She raked her fingers through her silky hair, then exhaled heavily as she leaned forward to stare at the blank screen. "I don't think—"

He caught her by the shoulder, the softness of her blouse under his fingertips, and he felt her tense at his touch. What in heaven's name had Elliot done to destroy his marriage and make his wife recoil at his touch? "I'm an officer of this company." He took a shot in the dark. "And I'm a stockholder. I'd like an explanation. I probably deserve one."

She didn't move. "Monday or Tuesday we'll know, and you can—"

He tightened his hold on her just a bit. "I want to know now."

"Money makes you very concerned, doesn't it?" she muttered, then jerked her shoulder away from his hand. "All right. I'll tell you. There's more than two million in assets unaccounted-for."

He drew back, closing his hand into a fist, and stared at the top of her head. "Two million?"

"Give or take a million," she muttered.

"What happened to it?"

She pushed the chair back, and he barely avoided being hit by it. When she stood, she turned, not more than a foot from him, and met his gaze. "I don't have a clue right now."

He narrowed his eyes, as much to ease the pain that was beginning to throb in his head again as to take the edge off the image of her in front of him. He didn't know much about business, but he had a sneaking suspicion that two million dollars didn't just slip through the cracks. "Who can we contact to find out what in the hell's going on?"

"Just leave it alone." He could see the weariness in her expression, the way the corners of her lipstick-free lips turned down. "I'll be sure to send you a wire, wherever you are, as soon as we find out."

Her tone grated on his nerves, and impulsively he reached out, cupping her chin. In a heartbeat, she struck at him, knocking his hand away from her, and her face flooded with color. He drew back, stunned by the pure anger in her eyes.

Before he could figure out what to do, the phone rang. The two of them stood there staring at each other. Then, on the third ring, Sean turned away from him and answered it. Mac watched her, the feeling of her slap on his arm still tingling, but not enough to make him forget the feeling of her silky skin under his fingertips when he'd touched her face. He heard her talking, and then she turned to him, the anger gone, replaced by something he could only call indifference. That was almost as shunning as the anger.

"It's for you," she said, and handed the receiver to him.

He closed his hand around the plastic handset, which still seemed warm from her touch, and watched her move away from him. Putting the receiver to his ear, he said, "Yes?"

"Charles? It's Paul," a man said on the other end of a static-filled line. "I know it's late there, but I was getting nervous." He paused. Then: "Is your wife still there?"

"Yes."

"All right, I know you can't say anything, just tell me if you've had time to sort through things?"

"No, not really," he said, without any idea what he was talking about.

"Do you have any idea when you'll know for sure?"

He pressed his thumb and forefinger to the bridge of his nose. "I don't." He watched Sean go to the window and stare out at the night. "I just got home."

"Let me give you a number where I'm going to be for the weekend, then you can call me as soon as you know anything."

"Just a minute." He looked at Sean and asked, "A pen and paper?"

"The drawer to your right," she said without turning.

Mac opened the drawer and took out a notepad and pen. "All right," he said into the phone. "What's the number?"

The man recited a number, then said, "As soon as you know anything, call, day or night."

"Sure," Mac said, and the line clicked.

Slowly he put the phone back in the cradle. "That was Paul," he said, staring at the number he'd taken down.

Sean didn't turn, just kept looking out the windows. "Paul Dupont, from the Paris office?"

"Paul Dupont," he said as he wrote the name under the phone number. "Yes."

"Why was he calling?"

"To make sure I made it home."

She turned, her eyes narrowed. "What is he, your personal bodyguard? Last time I looked, he was a simple accountant on staff there."

He backtracked to cover himself. "He still is. He's just worried about some orders, and he wanted me to check on things while I'm here."

She closed her eyes for a moment, then ducked her head and moved away from him. "It's getting late," she mumbled, and headed for the door.

"Sean?"

She stopped at the doorway, but didn't turn toward him. "What now?"

He looked at her slender shoulders. Tension was evident in the way she held her head. "I'm sorry."

She didn't respond for a moment, but then she slowly turned. When he met her huge amber eyes, he had to brace himself. "Why?" she asked in a low voice.

Because she was beautiful, and Charles Elliot had hurt her in some horrible way. "For touching you," he said, knowing the magnitude of that lie as soon as the words hung between them.

"What's going on with you?"

"I was just asking questions, and I expected you to tell me what was going on. I promise you, I'm interested, and I can understand it, if you explain it to me."

"I know you can understand it. You used to be very good at this business. I just didn't think you really wanted to know. That you were..."

"Just trying to annoy you?"

Mac felt his breath catch when she unexpectedly smiled, a mere suggestion of humor tugging at her lips. "Well, aren't you?"

"No," he said with all honesty. "I wanted to know what was going on."

The smile lingered. "Maybe the bump on your head changed you somehow?"

He touched the bandage and found a smile of his own. "Hopefully for the better."

"Yes, hopefully," she said softly, her smile faltering, then dying. "Good night."

"Good night," he said, and watched her turn and leave.

Mac stood in the empty room, his fingers touching the spot where she'd hit him. What was the saying about the grass being greener? He shook his head. For a man who had looked as if he had everything in this life, Charles Elliot had had very little. He drew the chair back and sat down.

He turned on the computer, and it booted up into a word processing program with a menu. He'd worked on a computer for a while in a shipping office in Boston, and he'd gotten a basic knowledge, at least enough to figure out program prompts and how to hit the right key.

He brought up directories in the program, and when he spotted a whole series titled FINANCES, with extensions that could have been abbreviations for cities, he went to the first one, FINANCES.NYC. He brought it up and found financial statements for the New York office of Warren International from the first of the business year. One by one he went through them.

He saw columns of figures that made little sense to him, but one thing he recognized was the debit column. One debit was over a hundred thousand dollars. When he traced that entry, he found it had been an electronic transaction, and the destination wasn't included.

Mac sat back in the chair, unconsciously fingering the bandage at his temple. His head was beginning to ache, a low, steady throbbing behind his eyes. Why had he thought he could step into Charles Elliot's life and find the life he'd never had? All he'd found was a life littered with bitterness and problems, and a wife who acted as if she wished her husband would fall off the face of the earth.

Chapter Five

Sean left her room at six the next morning, dressed in jeans, a loose blouse and thong sandals. She glanced in the direction of the guest room, then hurried to the stairs and went down quickly. She didn't want to see Charles right now, not after last night.

She went through the house to the kitchen, started a pot of coffee, then went to her office. She stopped in the doorway when she realized the light was on, even though sunlight was streaming through the windows. When she took another step into the room, she froze.

Charles was in the wing-backed chair behind the desk, his head back, his eyes closed, his hands resting loosely on the leather arms of the chair. She silently went closer and saw that the computer was on, the screen filled with figures she recognized as the quarterly report from the San Antonio offices.

She looked at Charles, at his lashes, dark against his tanned skin. A certain vulnerability seemed to touch his expression in sleep. Unguarded. That was how he looked, and Sean found it almost unnerving, but in some way incredibly fascinating, too. She moved a bit closer, studying him, from the suggestion of a beard that darkened his jaw, to the abrasion on his left cheek, to the way his dark brows cut over his closed eyes. A lock of his dark hair rested on the whiteness of the bandage at his temple, and she just caught herself before she reached out and brushed it back.

The last thing she expected or wanted was to feel . . . what? Protective? No, maybe she felt vulnerable herself in some way. She didn't know. What she understood was that she shouldn't be standing here watching Charles. But before she could turn and make her escape, his eyes suddenly opened.

Their deep blue was sharp and piercing. Lingering sleep didn't soften his expression at all. And Sean had the sinking feeling that he'd been awake all the time and knew she'd been there watching him.

She made herself keep eye contact—waiting. Then, without a word, Charles shifted, sitting up and forward, until his elbows were on the desk. He sank his head in his hands, and spoke in a muffled voice. "What time is it?"

"Just after six," she said.

He raked his fingers through his hair, then looked up as he sat back in the chair again. "What day is it?"

"Excuse me?"

"What day of the week?"

She shrugged. "Sunday. Why?"

He closed his eyes for a fleeting moment, then looked back at her. "Jet lag . . . the bump on my head . . . I lost track, I guess."

"You lost track of time, too."

He frowned at her and the action tugged the bandage to a skewed angle. "What?"

"You've been here all night, haven't you?"

"I guess so." He motioned to the screen. "Figures can be pretty boring."

She didn't understand this. In the beginning, Charles had been a workhorse, putting in long hours with the company. But soon after their marriage, everything had changed, and not just their personal life. He'd done what he had to do, no more, no less, taking time out to pursue whatever woman crossed his path. When he'd suggested a move to the Paris office, she'd been relieved.

His value to her and the head office had diminished to the point that it was almost nonexistent. Since he'd been there, Sean hadn't had any idea what his work habits were, except that he delegated everything and made plenty of time for play.

"You were going over the financial records?"

"I tried to, but my head's not really clear." He looked at her, his gaze slowly skimming over her. "Were you coming to work on a Sunday?"

"No." She backed up and glanced out the window at the clear July morning. "I was going to go for a walk on the beach before I started on the party."

"Party?"

"The Fourth of July party... this evening."

"Can't Helen take care of that?"

She frowned at him. How could he know about Helen? "Helen?"

"I thought she'd do a party for you, or at least take care of delegating things for you."

"How do you know about Helen?"

He stared at her. "Excuse me?"

"She's only worked for me for two weeks."

She saw the way he hesitated, then waved one hand to brush aside the questions. "The note you left for her. I saw it when I came home. I assumed she was the new housekeeper, or some sort of assistant."

He really did know as little about her as she did about him. "I've never had a housekeeper here before, and my assistant is still Valerie."

"Of course it's Valerie. I meant—"

"Forget it. I know the goings-on in this house are at the bottom of your list of important things to know. And as far as the rest of my life . . ." She let the words trail off, uncertain of why she was saying them, or where she was going with them. "Just forget it."

"I told you I was having trouble remembering some things. I didn't—"

She held up a hand—anything to stop this peculiar string of attempted apologies. The last thing she wanted from Charles was an effort to make nice with her. It only reinforced her suspicions that he was here for a reason, a reason that had everything to do with him, and nothing to do with anyone or anything else. And that truth depressed her. "Never mind, Charles, just never mind."

"Why are you up so early?"

She looked right at him. "I'm always up early."

He grimaced. "Another fumble, huh?"

Why should it matter if he knew she had the devil of a time staying in bed after the sun came up? It shouldn't, and she wasn't going to let it. She hadn't thought about Charles for most of the past year, and she wasn't going to let him bother her now. "It doesn't matter. I'm going to take a walk on the beach. Helen's supposed to be here at seven."

He stood and brushed past her, talking over his shoulder as he headed for the door. "Wait here. I'll be down in a few minutes."

"Wait for what?" she asked as he reached the door.

He stopped long enough to turn and look at her over his shoulder. "For me. I'll walk with you," he said, then went out the door.

"But, Charles, you never liked to...walk on the...beach," she said, her voice trailing off in the empty room. He hated sand and water and walking with her.

She slowly sank down in the wing-backed chair, felt Charles's body heat, still caught in the leather, and quickly stood up again. Nothing was making sense to her. Certainly not the fact that she was considering waiting for Charles to walk with her on the beach in the early morning. Or the fact that, if she let herself, she might even like the idea.

That last realization was enough to make her leave the room and the house, and hurry down to the beach by herself.

WHEN MAC CAME back downstairs, dressed in Levi's, a gray T-shirt with a school emblem on it and a pair of running shoes, he couldn't find Sean anywhere. He walked through the house, briefly checking the rooms. All of them were done in a style he'd have called a bit old-fashioned, in soft colors that seemed to fit in with the outside world around the house, and in fabrics that were decidedly feminine.

Finally he stood in the kitchen, a large square room with a beamed ceiling, smooth stone floors, dark cabinets and a breakfast area set in front of a huge bay window that overlooked the back lawn and the Sound.

He didn't know what he'd expected. No, he did know. He'd expected Sean to be here, waiting to go with him. He shook his head. His thoughts must be more muddled than he'd first suspected. If he was right, this woman merely tolerated her husband . . . from a distance. But he needed to be around her, at least for a while, to absorb all he could about his new life. He crossed to the bay window and looked out into the early morning.

To the right was a sprawling stone terrace with wrought-iron furniture and dwarf fruit trees in clay pots. He looked beyond it at an expanse of emerald grass that fell away toward the deep blue of the Sound. He went out of the kitchen and stepped into a sprawling family room with a built-in television near a wet bar, comfortable-looking leather furniture, a wall of French doors and soft blue throw rugs on a worn stone floor.

One of the doors on the back wall was ajar. He pulled it open to step outside into the morning. The air was clean and sharp, touched with a hint of the heat of the coming day, and a freshness that he could almost taste. Inhaling deeply, he scanned the terrace area, then saw footprints that had pressed down the damp grass bordering the area.

He knew Sean must have come this way, and he didn't hesitate before following in her footsteps. As he neared the edge of the bluffs, he saw a heavy wooden rail, then stairs that had been set into the sweep of the thirty-foot bank that went down to the beach at a forty-five-degree angle.

The beach was narrow, not more than thirty feet from the base of the bluffs to the water, a strip of silvery sand spotted by gravel. Not at all like the beaches he'd seen on the East Coast or in California. He hurried down the steps that looked as if they'd been fashioned from railroad ties, stepped onto the firm sand of the beach and looked in both directions. Off to the south, about a quarter of a mile away, he spotted Sean, a solitary figure blurring into the distance.

Mac took off after her at a fast jog, but slowed as he saw her approaching an outcropping of rocks that looked as if they blocked the end of the beach. But when he got within three hundred feet of her, he watched her go to the water's edge, then disappear around the rocks.

Mac sprinted for the rocks, then slowed as he neared the water's edge and saw Sean's footprints pressed in the damp sand. He followed the tracks around the rough rocks, past a Private Beach—No Trespassing sign that hadn't stopped Sean, and stepped out into a small, protected cove formed by steeper bluffs on three sides.

Sean was no more than twenty feet from him, standing by the tidemark, talking to a man whose back was to Mac. The stranger was in a bright Hawaiian shirt and baggy white pants, and his thick brown hair was pulled back in a small ponytail.

Mac stood very still. Without knowing who the man was, he didn't know if he should leave so that Sean wouldn't know he was there, or walk over to her and see what was going on. But before he could make that decision, Sean shifted and looked past the man's shoulder. She made eye contact with Mac, and her instant frown wasn't lost on him. He didn't move. He'd let her make the first move.

When the stranger turned, Mac was surprised at his relief at finding the man was actually elderly, maybe in his seventies, with a narrow, heavily lined face that sported a short beard and shaggy gray eyebrows. Mac hadn't realized until then that he'd thought Sean might be having an intimate meeting with this man. With her marriage a sham, he wouldn't have been surprised if she had someone else, but that didn't make the idea any less repugnant to him.

Sean moved to the stranger's side and called out, "Charles. What is it?"

He moved toward her, the sand firm under his feet. "I thought you were going to wait for me."

He was aware of the man staring at him, and he wondered if this man was her father, the man Charles Elliot had talked about as head of Warren International. He'd just have to wait until he had a clue to the man's identity, and hope he wasn't someone who could look at him and know he wasn't Charles Elliot.

"I didn't have time to wait," she murmured.

Mac made himself look directly at the man, and he found him staring right back. His frown drew the shaggy eyebrows almost together over his narrowed eyes. "So. Charles Elliot," he said in a clipped British accent.

Mac held out his hand, and was a bit surprised at how strong the man's grip was. "Good to see you."

The man drew back, his eyes narrowing even more. "That is a first."

"Excuse me?" Mac said, waiting for a clue he could work with.

"Charles Elliot says it's good to meet Barret Solomon. A first, don't you think?"

Mac stored away the name. "I'm sorry. I don't know if Sean told you, but I had an accident, and my memory has some gaps in it."

"You don't remember me?"

"Of course I do, but the memories are a bit foggy."

Sean spoke up. "So foggy you don't remember trying to buy Barret out so you could have this property?"

Mac glanced toward the bluffs, at the stone steps cut into the side, leading upward to thick grass and clear blue sky. It was beautiful, peaceful and quiet. Anyone would love to have it. "It's a nice piece of land," he conceded.

"Ever since Louis bought the place for you and Sean as a wedding present, you've been dogging me to sell it to you. And I should tell you that you can send all the wires you want from France, and threaten me all you want, but it will not make a bit of difference."

Charles Elliot had really wanted this property, and Mac had a feeling it had been for more than its beauty. More information to file away and think about. "Threats?"

"Saying you had lawyers working on the deeds on the island, as if you could find something that would alter my title to this land."

Charles had been hitting hard at this man. "I told you that?" Mac asked, looking back at the elderly man.

"Yes, and it will do you no good."

Mac looked at Sean, saw the frown that tugged at her mouth and eyebrows. She hated what Charles had been doing. He didn't have to be a mind reader to know that. And he didn't want her hatred. He looked at Barret. "Forget it. Keep your land. I won't bother you about it again."

The man looked shocked, and then, suddenly, he laughed. "I never thought a blow to the head would be so beneficial for all of us... unless it killed you."

Mac flinched inwardly at that statement, but tried to keep his expression neutral. "Well, sir, things change."

Barret kept the smile as he looked at Mac. "You seem to have, I'll admit to that." His gaze skimmed over Mac. "And for the better."

"Let's hope so."

Sean touched Barret on the arm. "Will you be at the party tonight?"

"Yes, I certainly wouldn't miss it." He patted her hand. "Now that your husband and I have reached a gentleman's agreement, I see no reason to miss the festivities." He looked at Mac. "I shall see you tonight?"

Sean shook her head. "You know he hates parties here, and he—"

Mac cut in. "I'll be there."

"I shall see both of you, then," Barret said, and turned to head for the bluff and the stone stairs.

Mac looked back at Sean as she watched Barret climb the stairs to the top of the bluffs, the morning sunlight etching her face with a clarity that made his middle tighten. Her dark lashes cast lacy shadows on her cheeks, and the sweep of her jaw and throat looked achingly delicate. And a truth dawned on Mac with the force of a fist to the middle.

Just because Barret had been a neighbor and not her lover, and just because her husband had been a jerk, that didn't mean there wasn't a man somewhere who loved this woman in every sense of the word. Then she turned, and Mac met her amber gaze.

"Why did you say that?" she asked.

"Say what?" He watched the way the light morning breeze ruffled her silky hair.

"That you'd be at the party tonight."

He shrugged. "Why wouldn't I be?"

"The question is, why *would* you be there?"

Charles Elliot obviously wouldn't be there, and he had an idea he should capitulate and say he'd make himself scarce. But he didn't. He'd decided somewhere along the way that if he was to have Charles Elliot's life, he wanted it to be a life worth having. And he knew right then that if he kept this distance between himself and Sean, if he kept their lives and interests separate, that life could be just as empty as his own had been.

"I'll be there because it's being given by my wife at my house."

She looked at him for a long moment, as if trying to digest his words. Then she veered away from the subject of the party. "Were you serious about what you said to Barret?"

"About the land?"

"Yes."

"I meant it."

"And you're going to be at the party tonight?"

"It's the Fourth of July, isn't it?"

"You know it is."

"I want to be there."

"Why?"

"I told you I wanted to be." He shrugged and tried to smile. "Maybe the blow to my head knocked some sense into me."

She came closer to him and reached out unexpectedly to touch his temple, where he'd put the smaller Band-Aid. "I forgot how you said you did this," she said in a low voice.

"I don't think I told you."

He stood very still as she drew her hand back and pushed her hands into the pockets of her shorts. Slowly she rocked back and forth on the balls of her feet. "Forget it. You don't have to. It doesn't make any difference. All that counts is, you're going to leave poor Barret alone."

"Was I that horrible to him?"

She cocked her head to one side and studied him intently. "Horrible? Yes, you were horrible."

"What did I do?"

"You know what you did."

"Humor me and give me a list. I'm sure you've got one tucked away somewhere."

She looked up and down the beach, then turned to head for the rocks. "Come on. I'll give you a list on the way back to the house. I've been too long. Helen's probably waiting for me."

He fell in step beside her, matching his pace to her shorter stride. "Well, what about the list?" he asked as they went around the rocks and back onto the beach that led to the house.

She kept her eyes forward as she began to talk. "One. You hated Barret living there from the first."

"Why did I hate it?"

"You just wanted the value of his land added to ours."

"Go on."

"Two, you like to get your way, and you've hounded poor Barret since the beginning to get him to give up his land. You wired him from Paris. You had the boundaries resurveyed, hoping to find that his property line infringed on ours."

"No wonder he's less than pleased with me."

She stopped by the water's edge and looked at Mac. "A lot of people are less than pleased with you."

"Including you?"

He saw color touch her cheeks as she turned to look out across the Sound. "Including me," she said.

Mac exhaled and looked down at the waterline, about two feet in front of him. Charles Elliot would never have won a man-of-the-year award. "I've been a pain, haven't I?"

"Yes." The single world hung between them, and as Mac looked out at the waters of the Sound, Sean said, "I changed my mind. Tell me how you got that bump on your head?"

He tucked the tips of his fingers in his pockets and told her the truth. "I'd just gotten into Seattle, and it was raining. I went into a bar to get dry, and I had too much to drink."

"Why were you drinking?"

He studied the blurred skyline of the city across the Sound as he remembered the night. "It was raining and cold. It seemed like a good idea at the time." He squinted at the scenery, trying to block the images from the night as they came back to him. "The ferry . . . I missed the last trip."

"Oh, so that's what happened?"

"What happened?"

"Whoever she was, she must have been something, to make you miss the last ferry."

Mac turned as Sean walked off along the beach, her head down, as if she were watching each step she took. He went after, hurrying to catch up, and when he caught up to her, he reached out to stop her. His hand closed on her shoulder, and he felt her flinch at the contact. But she stopped and didn't shake loose from his grip. "Don't I get a chance to tell you why I really missed the ferry?"

She cast him a slanted look that was unreadable. "You don't have to explain," she said, in a voice just above a whisper. "Our deal still stands. But it doesn't include you getting falling-down drunk and getting into God knows what sort of trouble."

He let her go, thrusting his hands behind his back to keep from shaking her. "Our deal?" he asked.

She turned to face him, folding her arms tightly over her breasts. "Don't tell me that you've forgotten that, as well?"

"What if I said I have?"

Her gaze locked with his. "It's simple, Charles. Do whatever you want with whomever you want, but in no way humiliate the family or the business."

"And you do what you want with whomever you want." It wasn't a question, it was a confirmation of what he'd thought earlier, when he'd first found her with Barret.

"Bingo." She tapped him on his chest with her forefinger. "You've got it. So you don't owe me any explanations. Just don't get drunk in public and get arrested."

"I missed the ferry because my flight was late," he said quickly, repeating the words Charles Elliot had said to him in the bar. "I wasn't with anyone, except for a man in a bar who talked to me and drank a bit with me." Strangely, in the image he had in his mind of that time in the bar, he was the one sitting in Elliot's seat, looking at Mac Gerard, wet, dirty, worn out from running. It shocked him, and he had to refocus his attention to finish. "I drank too much, and I fell on the sidewalk outside. It was raining, and slippery."

"If you say so," she said indifferently.

He hated the way she shut him out without even turning away from him. "Sean, this marriage—"

"Marriage?" she asked. "There isn't any marriage."

"Could there be one again?"

She exhaled heavily. "Charles, it never was a marriage. Not even at the first, not even when I thought it might be."

"Then would you tell me one thing?"

"I don't know if I—"

"Why did you marry me?"

She looked confused for a moment, and then she veiled her eyes by lowering her lashes a fraction of an inch. "You were excited about Warren's and working there, and you seemed to be good for it. I thought...I don't know, maybe that we could take care of things together."

Suddenly Mac knew exactly what the core of this marriage had been. The best interests of Warren International, the company her father had founded, the company she was involved with, the company that seemed to be at the center of her life. "So we were more or less business partners?"

She grimaced. "A miscalculation, obviously."

"Why?"

"After we were married, you weren't interested in Warren at all anymore. You're only interested in getting what you want."

"Which is?"

She rolled her eyes skyward. "Why are you doing this?"

"Isn't it about time to clear the air?"

She looked away from him and stared at the sand under her feet. "I don't know if it will do any good."

He didn't know, either, but he knew he had to try. "Humor me."

She looked up. "Do you really want me to say it out loud?"

"I asked. Tell me."

"All right. You asked for it. You wanted money, an easy life and the means to do what you wanted without having to take any responsibility for it. Isn't that right?"

She had Charles nailed cold. "Could be. Or maybe I wanted you."

She flinched at that. "What?"

Standing this close to Sean, Mac felt that no man could be with her and not want her. Just inhaling the freshness that clung to her, or feeling her heat, made him yearn for a closeness that he had seldom craved. "Maybe I wanted you," he repeated softly.

She stood very still, her rapid breathing the only movement besides the stirring of the soft breeze on the summer air. "No," she whispered.

"Yes." He reached out, framing her face with both of his hands, and felt the erratic pulse by her ear, the silky heat of her skin, and the softness of her hair brushing against him. No doubt about it, any man would want Sean. Slowly he lowered his head and touched her lips. The contact was cool and soft. She stood frozen under his touch.

As he tasted her, his whole being drew into a tight awareness that came swiftly, almost violently. It was all he could do to keep the contact gentle and to fight his impulse to pull her to him so tightly that she'd melt right into him. He traced her lips with his tongue, savoring a unique essence that stopped his breath. Slowly, as her lips parted, Mac slipped into a world where all he knew was Sean and heat and need.

He tasted her, his tongue sampling her moistness, and the kiss grew deeper and deeper, yet their bodies didn't touch, just their lips and his hands on her face. He felt as if he were inhaling her, as if a oneness that had seemed nothing more than a poetic statement before were a reality thrust upon him in a single beat of his heart.

Then her hands moved to cover his where they framed her face, and she drew back. Mac looked down into eyes that radiated with the same need that was making his body ache. Desire was heavy in her eyes, and her lips were parted and swollen from the kiss. It was like the dream, but she was real under his hands. The heat and need were real and vital.

Then, just as in the dream, she breathed, "Charles," and a bone-deep chill coursed through Mac.

Chapter Six

Sean felt as if she had been blindsided by the kiss. She hadn't seen it coming, not after the talk of their marriage—or the lack of it. It had been an effort just to say the words to Charles, to finally say out loud that their marriage had never been more than two people who had married, then found that they had done it for all the wrong reasons.

In some way, it had put her feelings in perspective. It had put a stop to the strange headiness she'd felt when Charles had walked by her, when she'd felt his body heat near her arm. Or when he'd stopped her by grabbing her arm. Even when he'd said he'd wanted her, she'd been able to duck the impact of his words.

But nothing had prepared her for the kiss. She hadn't seen it coming. She hadn't been ready for the contact, not for his strong, rough hands cupping her face with aching gentleness, and not for the moment when his lips met hers.

She'd stood frozen under the caress, her body alive with sensations that bombarded her, but the ability to move or even breathe had been taken from her in a single heartbeat. She'd felt his lips on hers, the caress of his tongue everywhere. When she'd felt his lips begin to leave hers, she'd found the strength to lift her hands to cover his.

She'd opened her eyes and looked into deep blue eyes that echoed the confusion and need in her. And in a horribly painful flash of truth, she'd known that she wanted this man in a way she never had before. Wanted? No, she needed him. She'd breathed his name.

But even as she wondered at the way her world had been turned on its ear, she felt Charles tense, then pull his hands back. She watched the fire of need in him leave so quickly that she wondered if she had just wished it to be there.

"Why did you do that?" she managed in an unsteady voice.

He shrugged. "I wanted to."

"You haven't *wanted to* for years," she said, bitterness edging her tone.

His gaze held hers. "Maybe I've changed."

That was the limit. First his concessions to Barret, now this attempt to get closer to her. Words that were simple—*I've changed*—were empty for her. The Charles she knew didn't have the ability to change...or the desire.

"Sure," she muttered, angry at herself as much as at him. She hated the weakness he seemed bent on exposing in her since he'd come home, that niggling idea that things could be different. "When cows fly."

"You really are cynical, aren't you?"

"Don't I have a right to be, after everything you've done?"

He narrowed his eyes as she spoke, almost as if he were trying to shut out her words. Trying to do anything but face them squarely. "You've got a right to be anything you want," he said. "So do I."

"And what are you, Charles? A con man, a womanizer, a liar, a user?"

If she hadn't known better, she would have thought she'd hit a nerve with him. But Charles had no conscience. That wasn't something you just developed in your spare time.

"That's how you see me?"

She hated the way her hands were beginning to shake, and she clasped them tightly together. "Yes."

The single word hung between them. Charles stared at her for what seemed an eternity before he reached out and tapped her chin. "Then I'll just have to make sure you change your mind," he said softly.

Where were the arguments, the protestations? Sean felt off balance. Change her mind? Had she been right from the first? Was Charles after something, something he needed, something he thought she could give him, and willing to do whatever it took to get it? Would he even stoop to making her want him?

She couldn't stand here, facing him, with no words to say. So she turned and walked away, heading back toward the house.

"Fool, fool, fool," she told herself mentally with each footstep she took. What made her so easy? What made her vulnerable to an egocentric, selfish, unprincipled man who had stopped being important to her a long time ago? Important? He'd become nothing to her but a nuisance, someone to deal with and keep happy so that he wouldn't interfere with her life or the workings of the business.

And now he was... She couldn't even think of a word to describe how she felt about Charles. Even when she sensed him falling into step beside her, she didn't look at him. She just kept walking.

"Sean?"

She kept going.

"When's the party?"

She bit her lip, then managed, "Seven." She stared ahead, thankful to see the stairs to the house just a few hundred yards ahead. "What's it to you?"

"I'll be there."

"Oh, no, you won't," she said.

"Is it casual or dress?"

She got to the bottom of the stairs and reached for the handrail. The cool dampness of the wood under her hands only added to the chill that had begun to settle deep inside her. She went up two steps, then stopped and turned, thankful to have the upper position, literally if not figuratively.

The morning sun was at his back, and he had his feet spread, his hands on his hips. And at that moment he looked for all the world like a pirate, with jet-black hair ruffled by the sea breeze, a strong, lean build, an attitude that was almost defiant. "Well," he asked, "casual or dress?"

"You aren't going to be at my party," she bit out.

"Casual or dress?" he repeated.

She found an anger in her that mercifully obliterated the memory of the kiss for that moment in time. "Charles, just go. Take the ferry, go to the city and find a diversion for tonight and tomorrow and the next day, and the next year and the rest of our lives. Just leave me alone.''

He didn't move. "I'm here. I'm staying.''

"So you can show everyone the new and improved Charles Elliot?" she bit out.

"Why not?''

She shook her head. "No. I don't have time for this nonsense right now.''

He stood his ground and didn't say a thing.

When the tension became unbearable, she muttered, "Casual, damn it," then turned and headed up the stairs.

By the time she got to the top, she was almost breathless. Without turning to look down to see where Charles was, she hurried across the back lawn to the terrace. Just then, her housekeeper, Helen Stone, opened the doors and stepped out onto the terrace.

The woman was in her mid-thirties, with bright red hair caught in a loose ponytail, a freckled face and large green eyes. Her T-shirt, worn with faded Levi's and leather sandals, had a cartoon on it of a harried-looking man in a lace apron, gripping a broom. Under it was the caption Housework—Not Just For Women Anymore.

"I was wondering where you were," Helen said with a smile, her low voice tinged with a Texas drawl.

Sean tried to smile back, but she knew her expression was probably a travesty of politeness. "I was walking on the beach, sorting things out.''

Helen spread her arms wide. "It's a lovely day for that—and, thank God, the rain's stopped. None in the forecast for the rest of the weekend, either, so your party is going to be a huge success.''

"Is everything taken care of?" Sean asked.

Helen nodded. "I just need to set up the tents and tables. The food's being delivered around four, and the special ferry's all set. I'd say your party's almost a done deal." She tucked her fingertips in the pockets of her Levi's. "How would you like me to dress for the party?"

The question made Sean tighten. "Casually." She glanced at Helen's T-shirt. "Something not too controversial."

Helen laughed. "Sure, something nice, like 'Go ahead, light my fuse'?"

Sean was surprised she could chuckle. "Rethink that one."

"Rethink what?" Charles asked from behind Sean.

Helen looked past Sean, and her smile grew. "Well, hello there."

Charles came to Sean's side, his arm brushing her shoulder, and she had to make herself not move away from the contact. "Are the guests getting here early?" Charles asked.

"Charles, this is Helen. Helen, Charles. He got in yesterday."

Helen moved to hold out her hand to Charles. "So, the husband returns? I'm Helen Stone, housekeeper and general flunky around here." Sean cast a slanting glance to her right and saw Charles clasp the woman's hand in his. His hand looked remarkably strong as it gripped Helen's. Then she remembered something...roughness.

She remembered there had been a certain roughness on his fingers and palms as he cupped her face on the beach. It wasn't irritating, rather almost intriguing on her skin. Charles with calluses? And she found herself wondering what he'd been doing the past nine months to lose weight and gain calluses.

For so long she'd just been grateful he was gone that she'd never thought about his activities. But now she found herself staring at his hand as it released Helen's. But it was gone before she could see the pads of his fingers. "Helen's got a lot of work to get the party set up," Sean said quickly, hoping Charles would keep walking and disappear. But he didn't.

"What sort of work?" he asked the housekeeper.

"You know, setting up tables and the tent we're going to use by the terrace. I've got a couple of men from town coming in—" She looked at the Mickey Mouse watch she was wearing. "They should be here any time now."

"I'd be glad to help," Charles said.

Sean turned to Charles. Charles offering to do labor? And she didn't miss the way Helen was smiling at him. Flirting? The idea was ludicrous. But then Sean looked at Charles. Maybe not. What woman wouldn't look at him twice?

The new, improved Charles Elliot? He wasn't really very different. A reasonably attractive woman could make him turn on the personality. Sean found bitterness rising in her throat. So much the same. What she didn't quite understand was why it made her feel so uncomfortable to see Charles smile at the woman.

The flashing idea that she might be jealous was squashed as quickly as it grew. Jealous? Jealous of what? "What could you do?" she asked.

The edge of derision in her voice seemed lost on him. "I can't cook, but I can offer a strong back."

Sean wondered if her mouth fell open, or if she just felt as if it surely would. "Charles, I thought you—"

"I don't have a thing to do until Monday, so—" he looked at Helen and said "—use me any way you want."

Helen laughed at that. "Wow, that's some offer."

"I mean it," Charles said.

Sean felt sick. The man turned on the charm as if it came out of a water tap. He'd do whatever he wanted to. She barely kept herself from touching her lips, the memory of the kiss coming back with such impact that she was having trouble concentrating on what the two people in front of her were saying.

"For now, I need to get the tables and chairs out of the garage," Helen said. "They were delivered Thursday, but it was raining, so we couldn't set them out."

"Garage. All right. I'll get started on them, and you can show me where you want them." Charles went past Helen and into the house.

Helen broke into Sean's thoughts. "The phantom husband is back," she said on a laugh. "And what a husband."

Sean looked at Helen. "Pardon me?"

"I'm sorry. I was just thinking that Mr. Elliot is certainly a very nice man."

Charles, nice? Had the world gone mad? "Nice?"

"Nice of him to help. And he's certainly easy on the eyes."

Sean was shocked that her first thought was to tell Helen that Charles was obviously married, but the words never were said. They sounded ludicrous even in her mind. And if he wanted to flirt with Helen, he could. She wasn't going to let it bother her.

"You're one lucky lady," Helen said.

"Sure," Sean muttered, and made her escape into the house. As she went through the door, she tossed over her shoulder, "I'll be in my office if you need me."

"Fruit, rolls and coffee are on the counter by the refrigerator," Helen called after her.

Sean went into the kitchen, and as she stepped into the stone-floored room she saw Charles by the refrigerator, eating a sticky roll. He glanced at her as he popped the last of a roll into his mouth, then lifted a mug to his lips. His blue eyes watched her, and she felt foolish standing in the door, wanting him to leave so that she could grab a cup of coffee and go through to her office.

He sipped more coffee, then rested his lean hips against the counter and looked at her, the mug held high in his hand. "The rolls are great. Want one?"

She made herself cross to the coffeemaker without looking at him, and was thankful that her hand was steady as she poured herself a cup of the steaming liquid. She glanced at the segmented oranges and strawberries Helen had put in a glass bowl by the plate of rolls, but didn't take any. With her coffee in her hand, she headed for the office. She almost made it before Charles spoke again.

"You need to eat, Sean."

She glanced back at him. "Are you serious about helping with the party?"

"I said I'd help Helen."

"Sure. Help Helen," she said, hating the tone of her voice.

He took his time drinking more coffee, his gaze never leaving her over the rim of the mug. Then, without taking his eyes off her, he reached back and put the mug down on the counter. "Helen seems nice, and I don't have anything else to do. You're going to be on the computer, aren't you?"

"Yes, but—"

"Then go and work. See if you can find all that money, and I'll help Helen." He reached for the tray of rolls and held it out in her direction. "Food?"

The idea of eating was making her feel a bit sick. "No, thanks," she murmured. Then she found herself saying, "Charles?"

"What?"

"If you're thinking of doing . . . anything on the island, don't. I won't stand for it."

"Do what?"

The raised eyebrow and the innocent look almost choked her. "You know what I mean," she muttered, and went into the office. She seldom closed the door, but this time she did, and she felt a degree of relief when the barrier was in place.

FOR TWO HOURS Sean worked at the computer, but her ability to focus on the information she was studying was pitifully low. She could hear voices from the back area—Helen, Charles, other male voices—and she finally sat back in the chair and hit the Save button on the computer keyboard.

She wasn't getting anywhere. She could trace the money links from branch to branch, but she always hit a dead end when she tried to find the route it took to oblivion. As she turned off the computer, she rested her head against the back of the chair and closed her eyes. When she had a sudden image of Charles kissing her on the beach, she quickly opened her eyes again.

"Damn it," she muttered as she sat forward and reached for the phone. Quickly she pushed in her father's number, and was relieved when Louis answered.

"Hello?"

"Louis, it's me."

"What's going on?"

"I'm hitting dead ends trying to trace the money. Have you heard anything at all?"

"I just talked to Quint. Nothing so far, but he and his staff are going to stay on it over the holiday." He exhaled. "What time is the party tonight?"

"Seven. You're coming, aren't you?"

"Of course. I've just lost track of time."

She fingered the cord on the phone. "Louis, you'll never guess who was here when I came home."

"The housekeeper with the T-shirts?" he asked with a laugh.

"Charles."

"What on earth was he doing there?"

"He came back a bit early."

"Is he gone again?"

She wished. "No, he's still here. He had a slight mishap and bumped his head. I guess he's going to be all right, but he's a bit foggy on some things."

"Such as?"

"Details." She wasn't going to tell her father that her husband seemed foggy on the type of husband he had always been. But not foggy when it came to women. "Nothing important."

"Then why do you sound upset?"

"This money thing—"

"No, it's more than that. Is Charles in trouble?"

She closed her eyes and spoke the truth. "I've been wondering that myself. Something's wrong, but I don't know what, and I don't have the time to play guessing games with him."

"What does he say is going on?"

"Nothing."

"Then forget it. What's the worst thing that could have happened? He got in a tight situation and needed space to let it cool off—or he wants more money."

"I guess you're right."

"Listen, I think I'll call Sweeney in New York and try to roust him a bit. Maybe he'll know something that can help us." He hesitated. "Sean, do you want me to come early?"

"No. Seven's fine. Just find out what you can from Sweeney, and I'll keep trying from this end."

"Sure. If I find out anything, I'll call. If you don't hear from me, I'll see you at the party."

The line clicked, and Sean slowly put the receiver back in the cradle. When a sharp knock sounded on the closed door, she drew her hand back and called, "Yes?"

The door opened, and Charles was there, shirtless, his skin covered by a fine sheen of sweat. "Helen wants to know if you want the tent right beside the terrace or farther out on the lawn?"

The sight of Charles made her throat tight and her mouth dry. The sheen defined his muscles and made him seem etched and lean. She'd never seen him like this. She'd never seen any man look like this, or had any man make her feel so aware of his maleness that she had to try twice before she could force words past the constriction in her throat.

"I...I guess by the terrace." She touched her tongue to her lips. "Or whatever she thinks is best."

He nodded, then looked at the computer. "Any luck?"

"Luck?"

"On the computer."

"No, nothing yet."

He took a cloth out of his pocket and ran it over his face, then down his chest. "I never thought it would get so hot here."

"It's July. Anything can happen. I was just wondering if you should be working like this, with your head injury."

"Actually, I feel fine now. No headache. But I did want to ask you a favor."

Her stomach knotted. Here it came. The truth. Now she'd find out just what he wanted. "What?" she asked.

"At the party, could you repeat people's names when they come?"

"Excuse me?"

"Their names." He touched the Band-Aid he had on his injury now. "I don't know if I'll be very good at instant recognition. So I thought, if you could just say their names, that'll help. I'd hate to look at someone, know them, but not have a name to go with the face.''

If she had been confused by the sight of the man in the doorway, she was beyond confusion now. ''You want me to say the guests' names? That's all you want?''

He nodded. ''That's it. I just don't want to offend anyone. Will you do that for me?''

''Of course.''

''Great. Now, I'll let you get back to work.'' He reached for the doorknob. ''One more thing, Sean.''

''What's that?''

''It might make things easier if you turn the computer on.'' He smiled at her. It was a full grin that lit up his eyes and made her stare. ''Back to work,'' he said as he turned and left, pulling the door shut after him.

Sean sank back in the chair with a shaky sigh, unable to get the memory of that smile out of her mind. God help her, she was cracking up. She knew that had to be the answer, the reason a simple smile could scramble her brains and make coherent thought all but impossible.

MAC WORKED OUTSIDE most of the day, taking time out only for the huge lunch that Helen had fixed. His head had stopped hurting hours ago, and he felt better than he had for a long time. No headache, no aches and pains, just fresh air and hard work. Best of all, despite the fact it was around eighty degrees, working outside with his hands helped to make his thoughts clearer.

What he was doing here seemed even more incredible as his mind focused. Yet it also seemed even more imperative that it work. In his gut he knew this was a last chance of sorts.

The two men who'd come from the town to work hadn't hesitated in accepting him as Charles Elliot. While he erected the tent with the two of them, he listened and stored away information. He found out about the island, about pirates and smuggling centuries ago. He learned about the opposition to a bridge ever being built to the mainland. And he learned what the locals thought about the people they considered outsiders—and that seemed to include anyone who had come here to live in the past fifty years.

As Mac finished getting the tent up, Miller Sabo, a middle-aged man whose family had been on Sanctuary for over a hundred years and who clearly qualified as a local, said, "Damn newcomers want a bridge, want to bring all the sickness of the city to this place. The hell with them," he said as he tugged at an anchor rope for the two-sided white tent. "This is a special place. Real special. No bridges as long as there's enough locals around."

Mac stood back. His shoulders ached from keeping the tension for the tent in place while the other two drove the support stakes. "I guess we're newcomers," he said.

Miller looked at him, then at the other helper, a kid of no more than twenty called Jerry Potts. The wiry, towheaded kid met Miller's gaze with a dark frown, then shook his head. "Your missus signed the no-bridge petition last year. I says to my dad, she's pretty good folks for a newcomer. Not like some up here on

Look Out, those that keep the places for summer, who just use the island, then trash it. Of course, she's a looker, and that don't hurt, neither."

"What about me?" Mac asked, wondering what the people around here thought of Charles Elliot. "What do people think of me?"

The kid hesitated, and wouldn't meet Mac's gaze.

"You can tell me," Mac said, not particularly liking Jerry, but curious about his opinion of Charles. "Go ahead, I can take it."

The kid took a drink of what had to be his sixth or seventh beer, then said, "My dad says that anyone who's out to take another man's property can never be one of us." He shrugged, reached for some loose rope and coiled it around his hand. "And you've been bugging Mr. Solomon for his place, and all."

"I settled that this morning."

"What do you mean?" Miller asked. "Solomon didn't sell to you, did he?"

"No, he didn't. I told Mr. Solomon that I wasn't going after his land anymore. I'm happy with what I have here." He looked out at the view, and at the blurred skyline of the city way off in the distance. "Really happy," he repeated, and knew it could be true.

"I'll be damned," Miller said, then reached for his tools and began to put them away.

Mac looked around the transformed back area of the house. About a dozen small tables had been set out on the terrace and the grass, with a long buffet table under the protection of the tent. Helen had kept busy decorating with balloons tied to the tables, the tent, and anything solid on the terrace.

She came over to the men, her bright red hair pulled back from her face. "It looks perfect," she said, studying the tent. "When the caterers get here, it's going to be simple to get things set out."

"Anything else you need done?" Mac asked.

Her freckled face was flushed. "Not out here, but you might want to try to talk your wife into taking a break. She's been in the office for hours. She barely stopped long enough to eat lunch."

"She's still in there?"

"She sure is."

"What time is it?"

She glanced at her Mickey Mouse watch. "Just before six."

"How long before the guests arrive?"

"An hour."

"Thanks," he said, then glanced at the two men. "Thanks for helping."

"Sure thing," Miller said.

Mac grabbed his shirt and headed for the house. He went through the cool interior, across the kitchen, to the closed office door. He knocked once, then turned the knob and opened the door. The interior was dim— the curtains had been pulled across the windows—and one glance at the computer told him it was off. No one was in the chair behind the desk.

He almost went back out, but then he heard Sean say, "What do you want?"

He looked in the direction of the voice and saw Sean sitting in a chair opposite the desk, near a wall that held plaques and books. He went in, leaving the door ajar, and crossed to the chair where she sat and looked down at her. "Is something wrong?"

She looked up at him, the dim light blurring her features. "Wrong? No, not really. Why?"

"You're sitting alone in the dark. Did you have bad news? Did you find something in the files?"

"I haven't found a thing, and I was just taking some time to think. What do you want?"

"You."

She sat very still. "What?"

"Helen said you hadn't taken a break. It's time you called it a day. The party's going to start in an hour, and you need to get ready."

"I'll be ready. I'd like to ask you something, though."

"Anything."

"Is this all some game? Some twisted way of getting what you want?"

Her words cut through him. *Was* that what he was doing, playing a game, getting what he wanted? He *did* want this life. That wasn't in question, and he knew he was selfishly going after it. But it was definitely not a game. It was life and death. "No. It's no game, no matter what you think of me."

She held out a hand to him. "Give me your hand."

He stared at her. "My hand?"

"Yes."

He dropped to his haunches by the chair, gripping the arm with one hand and holding out the other to her.

She touched him and gently turned his hand palm up. As she cradled his hand in hers, she touched his palm with the tip of her finger. Slowly she ran her finger over his skin, the contact as light as a feather, but as compelling as life itself.

"Wh-what are you doing?" he asked, shocked at the immediate effect her touch had on his body.

Her finger stilled. Then she raised her gaze to meet his. "You have calluses. The man I knew didn't have calluses."

Mac stopped breathing. For a heartbeat, he thought she finally knew. But when she caught his hand between both of hers, her palms pressed against his skin, she dissolved that fear. "I thought I knew you so well, Charles. But it looks as if I never really did, did I?"

"I don't think either one of us knew the other very well," he murmured, relief making his senses so alive he could have sworn he could feel each breath she took.

"No, we didn't," she whispered, and slowly let his hand go as she sank back in the chair. "Why was that, do you suppose? Work? Lies? The other women?"

Lies? That hit hard, about as hard as the idea that Charles had had other women. How could the man have looked at anyone else when Sean was right here? "Maybe I didn't know how to get to know the real you. Or maybe I didn't know how to make a marriage work. Or maybe we were so caught up in justifying getting married that we forgot what the real reasons *should* be."

"The real reasons?" she asked, her voice barely above a whisper. "Do you know what they are?"

"Love, caring, need. I think there must be a list somewhere."

She shifted and came closer to him. Without warning, her hand lifted to touch his face. Silky heat caressed his jaw as Sean breathed softly, "Who are you?"

He swallowed hard. "I'm me."

"That's just it. I don't know you. I'm not sure I want to."

The words made him wish that he had the right answers, that he could give her a reason to give Charles another chance. "What if I help? What if we start from square one and find out what makes each other tick?"

"I don't know." Her touch on him was unsteady. "Would that be safe?"

He'd given up thinking about safety a long time ago. "I don't know, either." He thought about the past twenty-four hours and knew the truth of those words. But right then he knew another truth. He wanted his new life to be with this woman. He wanted her to want *him*—the man he was, not the man she'd been married to before. "But I want to get to know you," he admitted.

When she didn't move, didn't say a thing, he skimmed his hand over hers where it rested on his face. Then he eased it under the silky veil of her hair to the nape of her neck, and drew her toward him.

Chapter Seven

Sean had done little during the day except stare at the computer and think about what had happened with Charles on the beach. And now he was here, his hands on her body, his mouth near hers. And this time she didn't freeze up. She moved to him, her arms going around his neck, her lips parting in welcome.

She didn't have a clear idea of what was happening between the two of them. She didn't even know if she could trust Charles, but she knew one thing with stinging clarity. She wanted him. Heaven help her, for the first time in all her married life, she felt a desire for her husband that overrode all sense and reason.

His tongue invaded her mouth, and she welcomed it. His hands moved on her back, to her waist, and the next thing she knew, he'd shifted so that he was between her knees, and she had the overwhelming urge to wrap her legs around him. Her fingers tunneled into his thick hair, and she tasted him with her tongue and lips.

His hands came around her waist, working under her top until she felt the tingling abrasiveness of his skin against hers. She gasped, arching toward him.

Her head fell back, and his lips found her exposed throat and a wildly beating pulse. When his hands found her breasts, she felt the world stop. When he cupped their weight through the thin lace of her bra, she moved closer.

She wrapped her legs around his waist, getting as close as humanly possible, and her mouth tasted his throat, the vague saltiness from the work he'd done, and a maleness that seemed to haunt her. His hand tugged at the material of her bra, freeing her breasts, and when his fingers found her nipples, she heard a gasp and knew it was her own voice.

Then another voice was there. "Oh, shoot, excuse me, I'm sorry..."

Sean felt Charles freeze at the same time she did, and when she opened her eyes, he was looking right at her. "What is it, Helen?" he asked.

Sean looked over Charles's shoulder at Helen in the doorway. "I'm sorry. The door was open, and I thought... Never mind. I'm out of here."

Charles never took his eyes off Sean as he exhaled and slowly withdrew his hands, tugging her shirt back into place. She moved back in the chair, pulling her legs to her breasts and wrapping her arms around them. Slowly Charles stood. He hesitated, then reached out and brushed her chin with the tips of his fingers before turning from her.

"Helen, what's going on?" he asked.

"Mr. Elliot, I didn't have any idea—"

He held up a hand. "Don't worry about it. What's the problem?"

She stayed in the doorway, and Charles was positioned between her and Sean. "The caterers are here, and someone needs to sign for the things. Either you or your wife.''

Charles turned to look at Sean. ''Want to sign for things?''

''Sure,'' she mumbled, and scrambled to her feet, going around Charles to head for the door.

She tried to meet Helen's gaze and act as if nothing had happened. ''Is everything there?'' she asked.

''I'm in the middle of checking right now.''

''Where are the caterers?''

''On the terrace.''

She felt awkward, with Helen, but especially with Charles. She made herself turn and look at him, and she felt her whole being respond to the sight. His mussed hair, his bare chest. The memory of his hands on her. She had to touch her tongue to her lips before she could speak. ''I'll take care of this, then . . .''

He raked his fingers through his hair, the blueness of his eyes hidden by the dim light. ''We both need to get ready for the party. We can talk later.''

''Sure, later,'' she whispered, and turned to follow Helen to where the caterers were waiting. And with each step she took, she felt a sense of loss that she couldn't quite define. Later. They could finish what they'd begun later.

MAC HAD BEEN Charles Elliot for less than two days, and he had already faced the fact that there were no rules. They were made up as he went along, out of the need to survive. It was the way he'd lived most of his life.

After a long shower, he sat alone in the silence of his room, thinking about this evening. He would meet a lot of people who knew Charles Elliot, and the idea of being found out wasn't at all farfetched. He already knew that if that happened he would leave. He'd walk away and disappear. And he would be right back where he'd been when he walked into the bar.

At 6:45, he left his room, and as he reached the top of the stairs, he was struck by the thought that he wouldn't quite be back to square one. He hadn't counted on Sean. He'd seen her picture, thought she was beautiful, but in his drunken haziness he hadn't really taken in the idea of a wife. It had just been part of the whole picture. Now he had the idea that she might be the center of the picture.

After touching her and kissing her, he knew he had to readjust. And he knew that a part of him wanted her to love him, to want him the way he could want her if he let himself. And that meant making this marriage more than a shell of pretense.

But could he afford to do it? Surely a wife, even a wife who was indifferent to her husband, would know if she was in bed with a stranger.

His hand skimmed over the rail as he headed down the steps. He *was* Charles Elliot. He was wearing the man's clothes, a cream-colored polo shirt, brown casual slacks and soft leather loafers. And he was going down to give a party with his wife. He had to keep up the pretense and keep his distance until he was so much a part of Sean's life that she wouldn't know the difference when they were close.

Tricky, he thought. And he knew just how tricky it would be to keep any distance from Sean, even for a short while. He went through the house, met Helen in the kitchen and read her T-shirt. Against a pale blue background, it sported a huge yellow "happy face" with a bullet hole between its eyes. A smoking gun lay below, with the words I'll Have Any Kind Of Day I Want To!

"Everything's ready," she said as she filled a huge punch bowl with pale pink liquid that had roses floating in it.

"Where's Sean?"

"On the terrace."

"When do you expect the guests?"

She glanced at a clock on the wall by the door. "Five minutes. Then it's party time."

Mac took a deep breath as he headed back through the house to the terrace. He stepped out through the French doors and saw Sean talking to a man dressed all in white. She wasn't looking at him, and he took the opportunity to study her openly.

Her pale hair had been piled high on her head, with wispy curls freed to brush her temples and the nape of her neck. White slacks were gathered at her narrow waist by a gold belt and matched to a simple white blouse of some soft material that billowed at the sleeves and had a low, full collar.

As if she sensed she was being watched, she turned. The blouse was cut low enough to expose the curve of her breasts, and the memory of the feeling of her under his hands came back to him in a rush. He quickly pushed his hands into his pockets and glanced around the terrace—anywhere but at her.

The sun was low, its lingering glow a golden hue that washed across tables covered with white cloth, each one decorated with a single red rose in a crystal vase. Balloons were everywhere, and twinkling lights framed the tent and the terrace. The table in the tent was heavy with platters of food, and a bar had been set up at the entrance to the tent, where white-jacketed waiters clustered.

"It looks great," he said as he looked back at Sean.

"Do you think so?"

"Yes." As she came toward him, he asked, "What about the fireworks?"

"The city has a fantastic public exhibition, and we just happen to have the best view on the island. It starts at nine."

"You've got everything planned," he said.

"I hope so." She shifted nervously, fingering the buckle of her belt, but when he started to say something, a horn sounded in the distance and Helen came out of the house. "The first cars are here."

Sean waved to Helen, then smiled at Mac, her incredible amber eyes shining. "Let's go and greet the guests."

"Sure. I'm coming."

She frowned at him, studying the plain bandage he'd put on after his shower. "How's your head?"

He'd almost forgotten about it. "No pain, but repeat the names, all right?"

"I will," she said. "Let's go."

He didn't actually touch her on the way into the house, but she was so close he felt her arm graze his, and a sudden sensation of being connected flooded over him. It was almost as strong as what he'd felt when they began to explore each other, and just as unfamiliar to him. He hadn't felt connected to anyone or anything for as long as he could remember.

MAC DIDN'T MEET Louis Warren until the party was in full swing. The fifty or so guests were scattered in groups at the tables on the terrace, people who ranged in age from twenty-something to sixty-something. And as they met Mac, not one of them batted an eye at his being called Charles Elliot.

After a couple of hours of almost holding his breath, waiting for something to be said, he finally let himself relax. He had finally figured out that Charles Elliot had had very little to do with his wife's friends. What would have been impossible if Charles had really been part of his wife's life was amazingly easy for Mac to accomplish.

Mac shook hands, had his back slapped in good humor, laughed with people who were total strangers to him, and stored their names in his memory. He met Barret Solomon, who acted as if they were long-lost friends now that the land dispute was over and done with, and he watched as night fell and couples began to dance to the music piped out onto the terrace.

Mac took a glass of champagne from a waiter and stood at the edge of the terrace, looking at the glow of the city across the water. When he sensed someone by him, he turned to see Sean not more than two feet from him.

"It's a remarkable night," he said, motioning with the half-empty glass at the night and the party.

"It's going well."

"I thought your father would be here."

"Oh, he is. He's in my office, making some calls, but he'll be out before the fireworks start." She looked past Mac, in the direction of the house, and smiled. "There he is now."

Mac turned to see a tall, gray-haired man coming out of the house. His dark casual slacks and open-necked white shirt looked oddly elegant on his lean frame. As he came closer, Mac recognized the man from one of the pictures in Charles Elliot's wallet.

"Louis," Sean said as he came to her and hugged her. "I thought you'd never get through with business."

As Louis Warren hugged his daughter, he looked over her head at Mac. As amber eyes identical to his daughter's met Mac's gaze, Mac could see surprise there, then something that made his heart catch. Mac had no doubt that this man knew he was an impostor.

When Sean moved away from her father to stand at Mac's side, Louis slipped his hands into the pockets of his dark slacks, but his gaze never left Mac's face.

"Charles was just asking if you were even here," Sean said. Mac stood still, feeling like a condemned man waiting for the moment when the noose tightened and ended his life. Or the swing of the ax that would behead him.

Louis Warren glanced at his daughter, his expression softening. Then he looked back to Mac. "I wouldn't miss a party of Sean's. But I must say, I'm very surprised to see you here."

"Charles insisted on being here. He's actually helped all day," Sean said quickly, as if she felt the nervous edge between the two men. "He helped put up the tent and set things up."

"Really," Louis murmured. "That doesn't sound like the Charles I know."

"Who does it sound like?" Mac said, figuring the best defense was a good offense. Let him say it. Let him get it over with.

Louis lifted an eyebrow and murmured, "It sounds as if you're a new man."

Why was he hedging and not confronting him? The nervousness that knotted his stomach was making him feel sick. "I guess I've changed," Mac said. "I don't think it's ever too late for a person to change, do you?"

"No, as long as the change is for the better," the gray-haired man said evenly.

Sean had stayed silent during the exchange, but Mac could feel the tension in her. This whole conversation was too close to the one they'd had earlier. And he remembered where that had led.

Louis looked at his daughter. "What do you think, Sean? Is Charles really changed?"

"I don't know."

"Any guesses?"

She shook her head. "No. I guess we'll just have to see what happens."

Louis touched her cheek, then drew his hand back, glancing at Mac. "I'll tell you what I say to anyone I'm doing business with. As long as everyone's satisfied, it's a deal, but if there are problems, it's all off."

Mac didn't know if the man was setting down his conditions for keeping quiet, or if he'd overreacted completely and the man was just a protective father. "I understand," Mac said.

"So do I," Louis said, glancing past Mac. "And there's Barret. I haven't seen him in months." He patted Sean on the shoulder, and then, without another glance at Mac, he went past them to meet the other man.

"Louis hasn't acted like that since I was dating," she murmured.

Mac finished off his champagne. "Fathers are very protective. I guess I would be, too, if I had a daughter."

Sean turned to Mac. "Would you?"

"I suppose so." He glanced at the terrace, then back to Sean. He really wanted to hold her, but there was no way he could . . . not unless they were dancing. "Since it's our party, don't you think we should dance?"

"Dance?" she asked as if the word were foreign to her.

He motioned toward the couples on the terrace, moving to a ballad by Michael Bolton. "You *do* dance, don't you?" he asked, hoping he wasn't way off the mark.

She shrugged. "Of course I do, but—"

Without giving her a chance to object further, he put his glass on a nearby table, turned and took hers to put it by his, then looked at her. Short of making a scene in front of her friends, he knew, she didn't have much of a choice, and he was willing to take that chance. "Dance with me."

"We haven't danced together since the wedding," she said quickly.

He reached for her hand. She showed just a trace of resistance as he laced his fingers through hers, then led the way to the terrace. When she faced him, she rested her free hand lightly on his shoulder, and with his hand on her waist he drew her closer.

For a moment he thought he'd made a horrible mistake. Being this close, feeling every soft curve of her body against his, was overwhelming. Even though she wasn't exactly melting in his arms, he marveled at how perfectly she fitted the angles of his body. Her hair tickled his chin. She sighed, and he began to move slowly to the music.

For what seemed an eternity, he felt her heat mingling with his, her essence filling his senses, and he closed his eyes tight. Every decision he'd made today seemed to be crumbling into ashes. Asking her to dance had been impulsive, and it had broken down his resolve to keep Sean at arm's length for a while.

All he seemed capable of feeling was the fullness of her breasts against his chest, the way her hips moved against his. He literally had to clench his jaw to keep from dropping a kiss on her bent head.

By the time the music stopped, Mac felt as if he had endured a self-imposed torture so exquisite it had left him half a man. When he felt Sean move back, when he met her veiled gaze, he knew that sanity was slipping away from him, the way it had earlier that day. And he knew how wrong he was to give in to the luxury of letting his desire dominate him. Above all, he had to survive, and he knew the end of this wasn't survival at all.

Willing himself to let Sean go, he stepped back and murmured, "I need to get something from the house," and he headed away from her before she could say or do anything else.

He didn't stop walking until he had gone into the house through the patio door, through the house to the front door, and out into the quietness of the deserted driveway. Only when the door clicked shut behind him did he take a relatively unrestricted breath. He moved down the steps, under the portico and out onto the front lawn.

His feet sank into the lush grass, and he inhaled the freshness of the night. Just then, someone called out to him. "Charles?"

For a moment he thought Sean had followed him, and he found himself wishing she hadn't. When he turned, he got his wish. Sean wasn't there, but a tiny woman with a dark cap of hair was heading across the lawn toward him. He'd met her. Sherri, or Sally, or maybe Sharon? He couldn't remember her name, but he knew she'd come with an older man, balding. They had plenty of money, from the looks of them.

He could visualize Sean smiling at the couple and saying, "Charles, you remember…" The name, what was the name? Then it came to him. "Charles, you remember Gerald and Sandi, don't you?"

"Sandi?" he asked as she came closer.

"Of course it's me," she said, her voice touched with a slightly nasal twang, maybe from Texas, or somewhere nearby.

"What's going on?" he asked.

She stopped a foot or so from him, and he could see that she was probably a few inches over five feet. The moonlight robbed the scene of any color, but he could see that her heavily made-up eyes were dark and had a slight slant to them. Her jeans and pale tank top were improbably tight, and she wore what looked like real diamonds at her ears and on her fingers. An attractive woman, in a flashy sort of way, Mac conceded.

"That's what I'm here to find out," she murmured, and without warning she stood on tiptoe and reached to touch his bandage. "Sean said you bumped your head."

"A small accident."

"Sean said you fell or something." Her finger trailed down the side of his face in an intimate manner that made Mac tense. "And I was so, so sorry I wasn't there to kiss it better."

"Sandi, I don't know what—"

Her fingers shifted to touch his lips. "Shhh..." She glanced over her shoulder, then back to him, and lowered her voice a bit. "I wanted to tell you how sorry I was to hear you got hurt, and I wanted to know if there was *anything* I could do to make you feel ... good?"

Mac closed his hand over hers and gently removed it from his face. "There isn't anything to do. I feel fine."

When he let her go, she moved even closer, engulfing Mac in a wave of perfume that all but choked him. "Boy, am I glad to hear that. I've been watching you all night and waiting to get you alone. You know, I always thought you were sexy, but you're even sexier now. A little leaner, a little more rugged." She pressed against him and rested her hands flat on his chest. "It's been almost a year, Charles, and phone calls just don't cut it."

Mac didn't need to have a building fall on him to know Charles Elliot had been involved with this woman. No wonder Sean had thought Charles would take off as soon as he got back to the island. She knew about the other women, women like Sandi. And it disgusted Mac that the man had gone looking for something outside of his marriage, something cheap and crass. He had been a stupid man at best.

Mac took her by the shoulders and gently eased her back to get some breathing room. "Sandi, stop."

"No one's around. They're all out back." She closed the space between them as she spoke in a low voice. "After you called me last week, I was hoping we could . . . get together when you got in Friday. But Gerald insisted on us going to some stupid corporate dinner, and I knew you'd be calling, and I wasn't there. We didn't get back until after midnight."

"I didn't try to call," Mac said bluntly. "I had other things on my mind."

She cast him a pouty glance. "Should I be offended?"

"We need to get something straight, Sandi. I'm married."

She was still for a moment, and then she actually laughed, the diamonds at her ears glittering in the light of the moon in the night sky. "Oh, Charles, what a joke. Of course you're married. So am I. That never bothered either one of us before." She tapped his chest with her forefinger. "And you've told me that Sean's a cold fish, that all she thinks about is the business, that she's boring in bed."

He hated what Charles had told this woman about his wife, and he heard himself respond tightly. "I have no intention of discussing Sean with you."

The pout grew. "You're a little late on that score, aren't you?"

He felt anger growing in him, anger at Charles and at this stupid woman in front of him. "Maybe so, but I mean it."

"All right, no talk about Sean. All I want is some fun." She smiled slyly. "And you have to admit that you and I *do* know how to have fun together."

"Sandi, forget it."

"Forget it?" she echoed. Suddenly, she grabbed for him, and then she was on tiptoe, wrapping her arms around his neck. The next thing he knew, she whispered, "Try and forget this, lover," and reached up to press a hard kiss against his mouth.

All Mac was aware of was the grinding of teeth on teeth, the sensation of drowning in heavy perfume, and her body moving seductively against his. But it wasn't close to seducing him. There was nothing sexy in the contact, and as Sandi gradually sensed his lack of response, she drew back.

The moon bathed her face in an eerie, colorless glow, shadowing her eyes, but he didn't miss the way her mouth tightened. "What's the matter with you?" she muttered.

He put his hands on her shoulders and firmly moved her back from him so that he could take a breath of fresh air. He'd never thought much about marriages; he hadn't been around them very much. But he knew that the idea of Charles Elliot sleeping with this woman was disgusting.

"I'll put this simply. Whatever was going on between us is over. Period. That's it."

Sandi grabbed his arm when he moved around her to make his escape. "You can't just walk away from me, Charles."

He looked down at her. The face that had been pretty looked hard now. Instinctively he knew that a man as selfish as Charles had been wouldn't let this woman back him into a corner. "Watch me."

Her fingers dug into his arm. "If you do, I'll—"

He tensed at the hint of a threat. "You'll what?"

"I'll make you sorry you did."

He didn't know how Charles would take the threat, but it only made Mac dig in his heels. He jerked free of her hand and moved closer, his voice low and tight with anger as he threw caution to the winds. "If you do anything to make trouble for me, I'll make sure you learn the real definition of *sorry.*"

He could see the uncertainty in her face. "What . . . what do you mean?"

"You like your life, your old husband, his money. I'll make sure you lose it all if you give me *any* trouble."

She drew back, her hands clenched in front of her. "I knew you were a cold son of a bitch."

"That's right. Now, just forget we were anything other than acquaintances. I'm married. You're married. Let's keep it that way."

"If that's the way you want it," she said quickly.

"I think that's the way we both want it. Don't you?"

"Sure."

"Good." Mac heard a high-pitched whistling, and then fireworks spread their vibrant colors in the air to the east, above the roof of the house. "The show's starting. Are you coming to see it?"

Without a word, Sandi turned and started for the house. As the fireworks bathed the night in beauty,

Mac watched her leave, and only when she was inside the house did he follow.

Thankfully, when he stepped inside, the foyer was empty. He went under the balcony to a small bathroom in a side hall and closed the door. He stood in the silence for a long moment before he crossed to the sink and turned on the water. He cupped the cool liquid in both his hands, then splashed his face.

As he looked at himself in the mirror, he saw a touch of lipstick still smudging his lips, and he grabbed a hand towel. Sandi had been right about Charles. The man had been a son of a bitch. Mac rubbed the cotton roughly over his mouth until all traces of the lipstick were gone, and then he balled the towel up and tossed it onto the vanity. With one glance at his reflection, he left the room.

By the time he stepped out onto the terrace, the guests were clustered in groups near the top of the bluff, sipping champagne and watching the beginnings of the fireworks show across the Sound. Sandi was standing behind the chair her husband sat in, her hands on the man's shoulders. She stared at the fireworks without looking around.

Mac saw Sean standing with Louis and Barret, and he crossed the lawn to them. When he came to stand by her, she cast him a fleeting glance that was unreadable before she turned away to look at skies exploding with a shower of colors. "I thought you were going to miss the show," she said to him.

Mac watched the way the colors played across her face, casting exquisite shadows at her cheeks and throat. "No, I didn't want to miss any of this."

He wished he could put his arm around her or even take her hand. But he knew that physical contact with this woman could be his undoing. So he stood with two feet of space separating them and turned his attention to the fireworks display. But none of the grandeur and beauty of the show could make him forget that Sean was close by, so close that all he had to do was to reach out and touch her.

Chapter Eight

For the rest of the evening, Mac wasn't alone with Sean, but watched her mingle with her guests, talking and laughing. When midnight neared and the guests began to shuttle back to the ferry, Mac was relieved. Especially when Sandi and Gerald Dunn made their goodbyes and left on the first van to catch the ferry shuttle.

Mac walked with Louis and Barret out to the portico, where the last van was loading. "Thank you for an enjoyable party," Barret said, and shook Mac's hand. "And thank you for being human."

Mac laughed. "I'm glad all the problems are behind us."

"So am I," the man said, then headed off along the drive to walk to his house.

Louis touched Mac on the shoulder. "I'm heading back on this shuttle."

"You aren't going to stay?" Mac had thought Louis would probably spend the night at the house.

"No, I need to get back. I want to be there first thing in the morning to find out what the accountant's learned."

"I understand."

Sean came up to her father. "Louis, are you ready? The ferry's going to be at the landing in ten minutes."

"I'm on my way." He gave her a hug, and with a glance at Mac he headed to the van and got in.

Mac stood by Sean as the van drove off down the drive and the taillights faded into the night. Then he turned to her. The moonlight touched her face, and he knew he'd better give himself some distance. But before he could make his escape, she turned to him. For what seemed an eternity, she just stared at him. Then she spoke, in a low, flat voice. "I know what you are, and I want you out of my house by tomorrow."

Mac understood the words, but Mac couldn't begin to assimilate them. Not after tonight. Not after he'd begun to let himself feel as if he had a chance of pulling off the deception and having a life worth living. "What?"

"You heard me. Just get out, or I'll have you thrown out."

Before he could say or do anything else, she turned away from him and went up the stairs into the house. Mac felt paralyzed. As she disappeared through the open door, he shook off his stupor and ran up the stairs after her. It couldn't end like this. He wouldn't let it.

Sean was at the top of the staircase when Mac burst into the house. He ran up the stairs, taking the steps two at a time. He caught up with her as she approached the doors to her room. When he reached out to capture her arm, she was prepared for it.

She spun around, jerking her arm free from his grasp. "Don't touch me," she bit out, her face stained with high color, her eyes filled with an anger that shook him.

Mac forced himself to stand there and push his hands behind him, clenching them into fists. "All right. I won't touch you. Just explain what you said down there."

Her mouth tightened. "Just what part of 'get out' didn't you understand?"

"The *why* part."

She bit her lip, taking a deep breath as a shudder ran through her. "All right. I'll spell it out. I knew you were here for a reason. I even asked you why you were here, but you never said. You acted as if you were my husband, as if we had some sort of basis for this marriage. But it was acting, Charles, just acting."

Charles? She didn't know. She still thought he was Charles, and she was furious with Charles. "Acting?" he managed.

"You *acted* as if you wanted this to be a marriage. You *acted* as if you cared about the company beyond what money it could give you. You . . . you *acted* as if you wanted me."

Acted? Heaven help him, but he wanted her so much his body still ached from the denial of it. "That wasn't an act," he admitted with stark truthfulness.

Her face tightened. "Don't do this."

"Sean, I don't know what's wrong, but—"

"What's wrong is, we had a deal. You agreed to it, and I thought I could at least trust you to keep your end of it. You broke it, so it's off. Now get out."

"No, I won't." He felt a certain strength, knowing she hadn't found out about his deception, and he wasn't about to fade off into the sunset just because

Charles had been an ass. "I'm not leaving. I just got home."

She came a half step toward him, and he could see her shoulders trembling. "This isn't your home. It never was. It was a place that was worth money, a place you wanted only because you figured you owned half of it. You leave, and I'll pay you whatever you want for your half. I don't care what it is."

"It *is* home to me," he said. That was what he felt. He was home for the first time in his life. Finally, a place to be, to live. And he knew he'd do whatever it took to stay here.

"I told you, you broke the deal."

"How?"

"You agreed not to do anything to embarrass me or Louis, or to damage the company in any way. In return for the simple act of being a decent human being, you got the job in Paris, the flat near the Seine, and free rein to do whatever you wanted to do...as long as you were discreet. You obviously don't know the meaning of the word *discreet,* so everything's off."

He was confused at first, but then, as he saw the color infusing her face, the brightness of her eyes, the reason for her reaction finally hit him. Somehow, she'd seen Sandi and him on the lawn. As the truth sank in, it made him even more sure of himself. Sean Warren-Elliot was jealous. She cared.

"You were on the front lawn earlier, weren't you?" he asked.

Her color deepened, and he knew he'd hit the bull's-eye. "Yes."

"Why were you there?"

"I was looking for you, to tell you the fireworks were about to start."

"And?"

"You were making out with Sandi Dunn like some sex-crazed teenager!"

A sex-crazed teenager? He would have laughed if he hadn't seen the touch of pain in her expression. "Why didn't you say something?"

"I wasn't about to lower myself to confronting you and your mistress."

He wanted to hold Sean and tell her how wrong she was, but instead he settled for crossing his arms on his chest and telling the truth. "Sandi is not my mistress."

"Charles, I saw—"

"You don't know what you saw, but I'll tell you what was going on . . . if you'll let me."

She shook her head and held her arms in front of her, palms up, as if to ward off his words. "Spare me, please. Just leave."

"I'm not going anywhere until you let me say my piece."

Her hands slowly lowered. "All right. All right. Just say what you want to, then get out of here."

"Sandi followed me out there. She had some idea of us getting together." He saw paleness begin to creep into Sean's complexion. "And I told her to forget it."

"Before or after you kissed her?"

"For the record, *I* didn't kiss *her*. *She* kissed *me*."

"Semantics," she muttered.

"The truth."

"Your version of it."

"Sean, I told her that whatever she expected of me, she wasn't going to get it. I had no interest in anything outside of this marriage."

The pain he'd seen a hint of earlier was back full-force. "Sandi Dunn isn't going to go away just because you tell me lies."

"Sandi Dunn is gone," he said. "And I'll make you a solemn promise. From this day on, I will never do anything to hurt you or make you jealous."

"Jealous?" she gasped. "Don't flatter yourself."

"Can you look me in the eye and tell me you weren't jealous when you saw Sandi and me?"

Her tongue darted out to touch her pale lips. "I was angry... and disgusted."

"And not jealous?"

"I was furious."

"And?"

"I... I was sick to my stomach."

"And?"

"Oh, all right, I was jealous... a bit."

He smiled at her. "Did it hurt you to say that?"

Her expression faltered. "It's... it's stupid. It isn't as if we have a real marriage. You've always done what you wanted to do."

"How about you, Sean?" he asked, remembering that moment on the beach when he'd thought, for a brief second, that Sean was meeting a lover. "Do I have any reason to be jealous?"

Color flooded back into her face, and her eyes shifted until she was looking at his arms, which were still crossed on his chest. "I have a life of my own," she murmured.

Suddenly their roles were reversed, and Mac was shocked to feel a raw emotion that he barely recognized as jealousy. The idea of a man holding and loving Sean made his jaw clench. The need to know the truth almost choked him. "Is there someone?"

She kept her eyes down. "What if there is? There have certainly been enough Sandi Dunns in your life since we got married."

He stared at her lowered head. Then he did something that he regretted almost as soon as he did it. He reached out and brushed at her silky veil of hair. He felt her jerk with surprise, and then, slowly, she looked up at him. No. He didn't want to know. He didn't want to hear about men loving this woman. Not when *he* could so easily love her. The thought stunned him.

In his whole life, he couldn't remember ever having truly loved another human being on any level. Yet he could look at Sean and know with simple honesty that loving her would be the easiest thing he had ever done in his life. And the most fatal.

If only she would move away from him and take any decision out of his hands, but she didn't. Her tongue darted out to moisten her parted lips, and it was all Mac could do not to pull her close. When she moved toward him, he stood very still. Then her hand touched his chin, her fingertips cool and seductive on his skin.

"Honestly, there aren't any men. There never have been," she whispered. Then she leaned upward and touched her lips to his. "Never," she repeated, then drew back. "Did you mean what you said?"

He couldn't for the life of him remember what he'd said to her, not when her hand was lingering at his throat. "What did I say?"

"That you'll never do anything to hurt me again."

His words, echoed by her, were almost painful to consider. Not hurt her? He'd do anything to protect her. But he knew that his lies had the power to destroy both of them. He had to keep the truth from her, if either of them was going to survive this.

"Or make you jealous?" he whispered.

"Yes."

"I promise. And I promise there won't be any more Sandis in our life."

"Our deal—"

"No deal, just a promise between the two of us," he said. "And as far as the company goes, I'll never do anything to damage it, either."

She was very still, and he could have sworn there were tears behind the brightness in her eyes. "Do you . . . do you want to stay with me?"

More than life itself, he conceded, but he knew that if he did he would break the promise he'd just made. If he went into her room and made love to her, the world would disintegrate around his ears. She'd know he wasn't Charles. And she would be torn apart by it.

He wanted her, but only when she could come to him with the same needs he had. When she could come to him, Mac Gerard, and not Charles. "I think we should take this slowly," he said, grasping at the safest course. "Besides, it's late, and we both need to rest. There's a lot of work to do tomorrow."

As he said the words, words meant to keep some protective distance between them, he could see her withdraw. And something in him could feel how much it had cost her to ask him to stay with her. He hated himself right then, but he couldn't do anything but exactly what he was doing.

She drew her hand back, and the last contact was broken. "You're right. It is late," she whispered, then turned away.

As the door clicked open, Mac spoke her name, surprised to find that his voice sounded normal. "Sean?"

She glanced at him over her left shoulder, lashes veiling her eyes. "What?"

"What time will you leave in the morning?"

"I take the seven-o'clock ferry."

"See you then," he said, and turned to go to his room. He knew he wouldn't sleep much tonight, not after what he'd just walked away from. But he could keep busy by going through the briefcase Charles had had with his luggage. Maybe he'd find something that would ease his entrance into the business world at Warren International. And maybe it would take his mind off Sean, sleeping just down the hall.

THE NEXT MORNING, Sean woke with a headache after a night torn by restlessness and thoughts that couldn't be shut off. Amazingly, few had to do with the crisis the company was facing. Most centered on Charles and what had happened between them.

First she'd been sent reeling by the interlude in the office, and then she'd been jealous. And it hadn't been the jealousy she'd felt when Charles flirted with Helen.

The emotion she'd felt was intense and hateful, and so foreign to her that it was painful to remember.

And Charles had known she was jealous when she confronted him, even though she'd hidden behind indignation and talk of deals. Then all the anger she'd tried to build against the man had dissolved so completely that in the end she'd actually asked him to make love to her. Not in those words, but she'd made herself plain enough. And he'd walked away.

While she dressed, she admitted to herself that she had never dreamed she would throw herself at her own husband. She'd never thought she could want her husband so much, or that it would hurt so much when he declined what she offered.

"Damn it all," she muttered as she stepped into the black pumps she was wearing with a navy business suit and a soft peach-colored blouse. She dragged a brush through her tangled hair, then caught the strands in a low knot, securing it with a pearl clip. After applying a touch of lipstick and mascara, she stared at her reflection in the mirror.

She looked pale, and the faint smudges under her eyes gave away her restless night. Determinedly, she added a touch of blusher to give her some color, and a spritz of perfume to try to lift her mood. But as she left her room, just after six-thirty, she knew it would take a lot more than perfume to get her to feel better.

She started down the stairs, her purse strap over her shoulder and her attaché case in one hand, the other grazing the banister. But when she looked down into the foyer, she stopped half a dozen steps from the bottom. Charles was by the door, looking up at her, and her surprise at the sight of him mingled with pure pleasure.

The pale morning light streamed into the space between them, defining him in a double-breasted gray suit set off by a simple red tie and a white shirt. His hair was slicked back from his face, and the bandage was in place. He was holding his briefcase as he looked up at her.

"I didn't know what time you had to leave to catch the ferry," he said while she made herself take those last eight steps and move toward the door and him.

"Why are you up so early?" she asked.

"I wanted to catch the seven-o'clock ferry, too."

She looked at him, saw the incredible blueness of his eyes under the dark eyebrows. "Why?"

"I figured we could drive together to the office."

"You're going to the office?"

"I figure I should earn my keep and try to help." He reached out and took her attaché case from her. "Do you want some breakfast?"

She found she wasn't really surprised by what he said. It fitted with his insistence on being at the party, and his insistence that she tell him what was going on at the company. "No, I'll pick up something when I get to the office."

"I'll eat then, too." He opened the door and let her step out first. She could feel him behind her as the door clicked shut, and as she looked out at the morning, she said, "I'll see you there."

"No, I'll ride with you."

He was at her side, the scent of soap and after-shave mingling pleasantly with the freshness of the morning air. "Why?"

"My head's still hurting. I don't feel like driving myself."

She didn't look at him as she started down the stairs and headed for her Mercedes. As she took her keys out of her purse, she hurried around to the driver's side and slipped behind the wheel. She started the car and slipped it into gear as Charles twisted and put their cases on the backseat. "I do still have an office at Warren, don't I?"

"Of course."

"Good," he murmured, and settled back in the seat, easing his long legs out and letting his head rest against the back of the seat. "There's a computer in it, isn't there?"

"I'd imagine so," she said as she got to the gates and pressed the automatic opener. "If not, you can have one brought in."

"Who orders them?"

"Elaine. She's been working there for the past six months, and she pretty much runs the executive of-fices." She glanced at him as they went through the gates and onto the road, heading for the ferry land-ing. She saw him rubbing at the bridge of his nose with his forefinger. "Does your head hurt?"

He closed his eyes. "A bit."

"Maybe you should see the doctor again. You never did say who you saw or where."

"A doctor at a clinic, and I don't need to see one again. I'll be fine."

Sean couldn't remember the last time she'd driven in a car with Charles, and she certainly couldn't re-member the air ever being so close, or her awareness of every sound and movement he made so acute. When she got to the ferry landing, the cars were just loading, and she eased the Mercedes into the outside parking lane at the rear.

When the ferry moved away from the landing, Sean sensed Charles shifting in his seat. "The locals like you," he said out of nowhere.

She looked at Charles and found his eyes still closed. "What are you talking about?"

"Miller and Jerry, the guys helping with the party, said that the locals think you're pretty nice." He rubbed his fingertips on his thighs. "I'm another story."

"They hardly know you. You haven't been around here enough for them to even see you, let alone talk to you."

"Just about the way I've been with you," he murmured.

She turned from Charles and stared out at the water. The docking site was coming closer and closer. "I suppose so." There was so much she hadn't known about this man, and not the least was his ability to make her act impulsively. Last night was the proof of that.

"What do they say about husbands and wives needing to be friends before becoming lovers?"

"We never were friends, were we?" And they had hardly been lovers. The perfunctory sex in those few months at the start of the marriage certainly hadn't been love.

"No, I don't believe we ever tried to be."

Mac heard Sean take an unsteady breath before she spoke softly. "I hardly remember what it was like at first. Even the honeymoon was strange, with me going on ahead, then you not able to come. We never did go back and do it right." She exhaled. "I guess we never wanted to."

He looked at her, at her profile. Her chin was held up just a bit. "Not a very good start," he murmured.

"We both had other things occupying us, I suppose," she said, squinting at some spot in the distance.

As he watched her, he had a thought that he was almost afraid to voice. But he found the words and asked, "Do you think we have the potential to be friends?"

She turned to him as the ferry slid into the docking channel and the motors stilled, then reversed. He met her amber gaze, and her next words gave him a glimmer of hope that this life he'd taken over could actually be his in every sense of the word. "I hope so."

For a moment he wished he hadn't walked away from her the night before. But the past was the past. It was what was ahead that counted. God, he hoped they could be friends, and he wanted to do this right. He wanted to start at the beginning with her, not jump in in the middle.

"Maybe what we need to do is date," he said. Her eyes widened, and that made him smile, partly from amusement at her reaction, and partly because he was feeling more and more sure that what he'd done had been right. "You remember dating, don't you? I ask you out, and you say yes, hopefully, and I take you someplace fancy, and we dance and drink champagne. Or we can go on a picnic and eat greasy chicken and watermelon. And we tell each other stories and secrets from our childhoods.''

The ferry stopped, and Sean didn't speak as she inched the car forward onto the dock. As she pulled up the incline and onto the street, Mac couldn't take the silence. ''Well, what do you think?''

She swung left on the street. ''It's been a long time since I had a date, and I was never very good at it.''

The street in the light of day seemed so different to him from the way it had been in the night and rain, when he'd been running scared. Cars seemed to be everywhere, and people walked casually along the sidewalk. As they neared the street where the Belly Up Bar and Grill was, Mac averted his eyes. He didn't want to see it, even in passing. Sean's golden hair and lovely profile were much more welcome sights. ''It's not a test, just a way to start, a way to figure out where we're going.''

She considered his words for a long moment, then nodded. ''All right. Let's do it.''

He found that a smile came easily, from real pleasure at her agreement. ''How about lunch, today? I'll take you out someplace fancy, and we'll—''

''Oh, I can't. Not today.'' She fingered the steering wheel. ''I can't leave the office, not with what's going on. I'll just have to grab a bite at the office.'' She looked at Mac. ''I'd like to, but later, when this is settled. Before you go back to Paris.''

He knew then what he needed to tell her. ''I've decided I want to get involved here at the Seattle offices. I'd like Louis to get someone else to take over for me in Paris, and I'll figure out where I can fit in here.''

She slowed the car and turned her amber gaze on him. "You aren't going back to Paris?"

"No, I've decided to stay home for a while."

"I thought..." She looked at the street ahead of her again. "Are you sure?"

He had an idea just how Charles had gotten the Paris job. "I know I manipulated things to get sent to Paris, but I think someone else could take over."

She swung right, onto a street lined with skyscrapers. "Talk to Louis about it, if you're sure this is what you want."

"I'm sure."

She signaled a right turn, then turned onto a cement ramp that angled down toward an underground parking garage for a glass-and-steel building that soared at least twenty stories above the street. In gold lettering on black glass Mac saw Warren International and a street address as they drove past open security gates and into the low-ceilinged garage.

He sat straighter as they passed a garage attendant, who waved to Sean. She drove the car into a space marked Management, right next to a series of elevator doors. She stopped the engine, but when she would have gotten out, Mac stopped her. "Sean, I need to ask you something before we go in."

She turned to look at him, her hand on the door handle. "What is it?"

"I know I haven't been here for a while, and the people who work here..."

"Oh, don't worry. They'll get used to you being here. If it works out, you won't have a problem. And you've got an edge."

"What's that?"

"Most of them don't even know you. I bet there are only two or three who have even met you before."

As the pieces fell into place, Mac felt a strange sadness that a man's life could be taken over so completely. That no one knew the real Charles Elliot well enough to know the difference—not even his wife. "Who's here that I'll know?"

"Stella Wong, Louis's secretary, although I think it's been two or three years since she last saw you. Jeb Renoldi, in the sales department, and the accountant, Orin Quint. Not many."

"It's as if I've got a clean slate."

"Yes, I guess so. Are you ready?"

He nodded and got out, meeting Sean at the back of the car to hand her her attaché case. Then he walked with her to the elevators, near the side of the low-ceilinged space. When the doors slid back, he and Sean stepped inside and started upward. Mac stood by Sean's side, and he could see their reflections in the brass interior of the elevator. A tall man with dark hair, a gray suit, and an incredibly beautiful woman at his side.

There wasn't a trace of Mac Gerard, with his torn Levi's, his heavy work boots, and the weariness that had etched his face for most of his life. He tugged at his cuffs, and when the doors slid open, he hesitated only long enough to let Sean get off first. Then he stepped into the world of Warren International.

Chapter Nine

Sean was distracted all morning, and it was the worst possible time to lose her concentration. Louis had brought her a stack of readouts to go through, and by the time noon neared, her eyes burned and her shoulders ached. Figures ran into figures, and nothing made sense to her.

Especially her own thought processes.

Charles mingled with every thought she had, business or otherwise. Dating? She could almost smile at that, but the smile didn't come when she realized she didn't just want to be friends with her husband, not when his mere presence made her want to touch him and be touched.

Maybe she'd gone about marriage backward, but she knew now that she wanted Charles—the Charles who had been with her for the past few days.

A sharp knock on her door startled her, and she called out, "Come in."

Meg, the secretary who had been assigned to help Charles settle in, looked into the room. "What is it, Meg?"

"I'm sorry to disturb you, ma'am, but Mr. Elliot

would like you to come to his office as quickly as possible.''

Sean stood. "What's wrong?"

"He didn't say, just that he needs you in his office right away."

As Sean reached for the phone to call Charles, Meg stopped her. "I don't think a call will do. He said he needs you in person."

"Okay." Sean smiled slightly at Meg's choice of words. She got up and went around the desk to go to the door. Meg backed up and fell in step with Sean as she went through the reception area and out into the hallway. Charles had his old office at the end of the corridor, a corner office that had been empty for years.

Once she'd arranged for Meg to work with him, she'd left for her own office. "He didn't say what's wrong?" she asked as they headed toward his closed door.

"No, he just said—"

"I know, he needs to see me."

"Yes, ma'am, that's what he said."

When Sean reached the door, she opened it without knocking. As the door hit the wall with a soft thud, Sean stepped right into the office. She expected to find a crisis thrown at her. But the beige-on-beige office, with its pale modern furniture and its stark abstract paintings in blues and greens, was calm and quiet. Boring, she'd always thought, but Charles hadn't liked clutter or details surrounding him.

Then she looked to her left and was taken back to see a great deal of clutter. A red plaid blanket had been spread on the carpet in front of the curtainless floor-to-ceiling windows overlooking Seattle. A large wicker basket with a bottle of champagne and two glasses on top of it sat by the blanket, along with a bouquet of red roses that had been arranged in a water pitcher. She could catch a hint of the roses sweetening the air.

As the door swung shut with a click, Sean saw Charles. His jacket and tie were gone. The sleeves of his white shirt were rolled up, and the top two buttons were undone. When their eyes met, he smiled. It was an easy expression, but it was still enough to make her breath catch.

"So, how do you like it?" he asked.

She stared at him. "I don't understand. Meg said there was an emergency."

"Since you don't have time for a date, I brought the date to you. And this is an emergency of sorts. Our *first* date."

She hid a distinct feeling of pleasure. "I thought you'd found something about the disappearing money, or that you'd figured something out."

"I've been trying, but nothing so far. So, I decided we both needed a break. Business is one thing, but you need to take time to smell the roses . . . so to speak."

She looked at the blanket again. "Where did this all come from?"

"Meg found a place that makes greasy chicken and watermelon. The roses are from the gift shop down in the lobby. I'm not sure what red roses mean, but I thought they were beautiful. The champagne proba-bly isn't a good year, but it's got bubbles."

He picked up the champagne, then poured it into the glasses. "It's not a perfect picnic without ants and the possibility of rain, but—" he put the bottle back

in the bucket, then came to Sean to hold out one of the
glasses to her ''—it's a matter of working with what's
available.''

She took the cool glass and trembled when she felt
Charles's fingers brush hers. Then the contact was
gone, and she cradled the goblet in both hands to
steady it. ''I never would have guessed that you were
so...so...''

''Impulsive?'' he asked.

She met his gaze. The blueness of his eyes was deep,
incredible. ''Yes.''

''Romantic?''

''I guess so.''

''When a man misses his own honeymoon, he
doesn't exactly qualify for the romantic-of-the-year
award, does he?'' He held up his glass. ''To dating and
being friends.''

He tapped the rim of her glass with his, and the
ringing sound echoed in the room. His blue eyes held
her gaze, and the world seemed to narrow to just the
two of them. Business pressures and worries were all
outside. Inside, it was just her and Charles and a picnic on plush carpeting.

He glanced at the untouched champagne in her
hand, then his gaze met hers again. ''You will stay,
won't you?''

She couldn't remember Charles trying to talk her
into anything, except when he wanted something or he
needed her help. He had certainly never tried to get her
to spend time with him. Days ago she would have
walked out on him and gone back to work. But she
didn't want to now.

''I can stay for a while,'' she said.

"Good. I couldn't possibly eat all this chicken alone."

He went back to the basket, taking the roses and the champagne bucket off it, then opening the lid. He took out a plastic container filled with chicken and put it on the blanket, along with a dish of potato salad and a dish of watermelon chunks. "They didn't have a whole melon, but I thought these would do in a pinch." He looked up at her. "Sit and enjoy."

She moved to the blanket's edge, then slipped off her shoes and sank down, sitting back on her heels. She *was* hungry. She'd never gotten the breakfast she'd talked about, and cups and cups of coffee were making her stomach rumble.

Charles offered her a paper plate and some plastic utensils, then sat opposite her, Indian-style. He helped himself to chicken and salad. As he speared a chunk of watermelon, he looked at Sean. "Aren't you hungry?"

"Yes. Yes, I am." She shrugged and took a sip of her champagne. "This is all so strange. Picnicking inside, looking down at the city."

"There's no rule that picnics have to be outside." He pushed the dish with the chicken closer to her. "That's the usual way, but if you eat food served on a plaid blanket, that's officially a picnic."

"I'll take your word for it." She chose a piece of chicken, then took a scoop of potato salad. "I don't think I've ever been on a real picnic, so you can do anything you'd like. I wouldn't know the difference."

He laughed. She liked the sound of his laugh, and could feel herself relaxing. "That gives us something to think about," he murmured.

She looked at Charles and knew her face was warming. "I didn't mean—"

"I did," he said. "But I was really wondering how you could go through an American childhood and never go on a picnic."

"I just never got around to it." She looked down at the plate resting on her lap and pushed her salad around with her plastic fork. "You know Louis and I weren't exactly like the Cleavers."

"Exactly how would you explain your life with your father?"

She took a taste of the salad, and wondered how the question could bring back the sharp edges from her childhood. She swallowed, then reached for her glass again. "You know there was just the two of us after my mother died." She swallowed more of her drink. "As far back as I can remember, there was the business."

"Didn't Louis ever think of remarrying?"

"I guess he must have, but the business always came first. I thought it was because he was so madly in love with my mother that when she died he didn't want anyone else." She laughed. It was a short, nervous sound. "If the truth be told, he's a workaholic. It's that simple. There's really nothing romantic about it."

"Maybe you're wrong. Maybe he had a love so complete that once it was gone he never looked for it again."

What had Louis said to her during the storm about there having been passion and love and caring when he was married to her mother? Had he told Charles the same things? "Louis told you that?"

"No. I was just wondering."

She stared down into her glass, at the bubbles that floated to the surface and burst. Was love an illusion like that, bursting when it was touched by reality? "I know he cared a lot." She looked at Charles, meeting his direct gaze and feeling the heat rising in her face again. "Why are you asking about it?"

He took his time answering. "I've been thinking about what happened with us. I thought maybe your father's ideas about love were the same as yours."

Louis had asked her about grandchildren. He obviously had had an idea that she and Charles could make this a marriage. How could he have a clue about that, when she would have wished Charles off the face of the earth just a few days ago? "Louis has his own ideas, and so do I."

She was certain he'd ask her what her ideas were, but he didn't. Instead, he asked, "Why do you call him Louis, instead of Dad or Father?"

If she hadn't known better, she would have thought Charles had been eavesdropping on that early-morning conversation between her and her father. "I called him Daddy when I was a child, but he's been Louis to me since I came to work here." She wanted to change the direction of the conversation. "What did you call your parents?"

He drained the last of his champagne and put the glass on top of the chest. "The usual."

"You never told me much about your family, except that you were an only child and your parents were killed when you were nineteen. You put yourself through college, hired on at Warren, and the rest is history. You have no relatives to speak of or to speak to, as you put it."

"You covered everything," he said as he sat back and looked at her.

"You hate to talk about your past. Why?"

"It's not worth talking about," he said.

"I thought your idea of a date was talking about our childhoods."

He speared a piece of watermelon with his plastic fork and stared at it. "All right, you got me. What do you want to know?"

"How about the best memory from your childhood?"

He exhaled. "The best?"

"The very best."

"I honestly don't remember a great deal. I'm one of those people who know they were a kid, but they don't have a lot of details."

"Then tell me something in general."

Mac popped the watermelon into his mouth and chewed, letting the coolness slip down his throat. A memory. He couldn't begin to come up with a fabricated one for Charles Elliot, so he found a memory out of his own blurred childhood, a childhood he'd tried for years to forget completely.

He swallowed the fruit, then shrugged. "All right. Eating ice cream on a hot summer evening."

"Who were you with?"

"A couple... I forget their names." A lot of foster parents had come and gone from his life after he was put in the system at the age of seven. "But I remember they had a dog." He remembered wishing the dog were his. "Big, black and brown, probably part German shepherd. His name was Tanner, and he chased fireflies. We stayed out in the yard on the grass until the ice cream was gone and the mosquitoes got so bad we had to go inside.''

''Where were your parents?''

''I don't remember,'' he said, hedging. ''I can't even tell you where it was, exactly.''

''How old were you?''

Birthdays hadn't been something worth remembering, either. ''I don't know. Young, pretty young.'' He poured a little more champagne for himself and drank some, wishing to change the subject. Enough was enough. He didn't want his memories intruding in this place. ''Your turn.''

She put her plate down on the blanket. ''The best memory I have? Louis and I lived in the house he has now. You've seen the banister there. It's terrific, with a curve in the middle, then a curled end. Louis told me never to ride it, which was like dangling a strawberry in front of a donkey. I *had* to ride it. One day when he was at work, I went down, and lost it at the end and landed on the floor. I was in the hospital for a couple of days.''

He couldn't help but smile. ''That's your *best* memory?''

''No, but maybe it's my most important memory.''

''How so?''

''Louis told me that any time I started something, I had to make sure I could see the ending, so I wouldn't fly off into trouble.''

That was something he had never done. He just went forward, doing what he had to do, without regard to the ending of it. ''How can we ever know the endings to what we begin in this life?''

"I don't suppose we can. Who knows the future? Four years ago, when we got married, I thought we would be a fantastic business team. Look how wrong I was."

"Maybe we had the wrong concept of the future." His hands cradled the glass. "Maybe when we see a chance to change our lives, we need to take it. Maybe that's the only thing that saves our lives, that ability to see an opportunity and take it and survive."

"That sounds opportunistic."

"Of course it does, because it is," he admitted bluntly. "But if you survive and things get better, is that wrong?"

"I suppose that philosophy is a key to good business."

She glanced at the wall clock and began to get up. He spoke quickly. "It can wait."

She looked back to him. "Excuse me?"

He didn't want her leaving yet. "The business can wait. The problem isn't going to get any worse if you take an hour away from it." He motioned to the food. "You've got ten minutes left." He could see her hesitating, weighing the options. "You're a lot like Louis, aren't you?"

She frowned. "I am?"

"A certifiable workaholic." He smiled. "You need to learn to take time for yourself."

She sank back on the carpet. "Ten minutes," she agreed, then reached for her plate, and Mac picked his up again. When he was finished eating, he looked at Sean as she finished off the last of her chicken and reached for a napkin.

She looked at the clock, then at Mac. "If I could cook, I'd make you a picnic someday. But you know what a disaster I am in the kitchen."

"I doubt you're a disaster anywhere," he said.

Color touched her cheeks, and Mac found he liked to see her blush. "I'm going to be one this afternoon if I have any more champagne."

"I was just thinking about the island."

"That's a sudden change of subject."

"Sorry. I was just wondering if you ever told me how it got its name."

"I thought you must have known."

"I don't remember if I did."

"A pirate named Fontaine found the island on one of his forays and took it over. It was his sanctuary, a place he could feel safe from retribution for his attacks on unsuspecting vessels, and the name stuck."

"A place to feel safe," he repeated. "Those places are few and far between in this world."

"I know. The first time I saw the island and the house, I knew I wanted to live there forever. When Louis bought the house for us as our wedding gift, I felt so grounded." She narrowed her eyes on Mac and almost grimaced. "I never understood why you didn't feel like that."

But that was *exactly* how he felt. "Maybe I was too worried about other things then. Maybe I wasn't ready for it."

"You would have been happier if Louis had bought us a condo in the city."

"And I would have been a fool. No condo has a view like the island house does."

"You can't beat the view," she murmured, then glanced at the clock. "Now I really need to get back to my office." She shook her head. "It's as if that money dissolved into thin air, but that just doesn't happen."

"Is there any possibility there was a bookkeeping error?" he asked as he got to his feet.

"Unfortunately not." She reached for her shoes and slipped them on, and when she would have stood, Mac moved around to offer her his hand. When her fingers closed around his, he drew her to her feet, and as they stood facing each other, he kept his hold on her.

"So, how was the date?" he asked softly.

"We didn't dance, and this isn't fancy, but I'd say it was a picnic with greasy chicken and watermelon. It was fine."

"Just fine?"

"Very good."

"Just very good?"

She smiled up at him, a light in her eyes that made his breathing constrict. "It's the best picnic I ever had."

He laughed. "Since it's your first, it has to be your best."

"If it was my twentieth, it would have been my best," she said.

The clock chimed the hour, but Mac didn't take his eyes off Sean. A friendship with this woman seemed so improbable. He had to take it slow, to build up a relationship. When they were together, it had to be because they *both* wanted it more than anything.

"A good start for a friendship," he said. It was hard to keep his perspective, with her so close he could feel each breath she took. Recklessly he reached out and gently traced the line of her jaw with the tip of his finger. "I want to be your friend, Sean."

"I want that, too," she whispered unsteadily.

His finger stilled on her check, and then he gently cupped her chin. And for all the wrong reasons, he did the one thing he'd wanted to do since the last time she was this close to him. He lowered his head and gently touched his lips to hers.

He wondered if there had ever been lips as soft, or another woman who fitted so neatly against his body. Every angle and curve fitted him, and it was as if she had been made just for him. He knew how foolish that idea was, but it seemed so logical when she was this close, when her arms slid slowly around his neck, when her lips opened to his.

When the phone rang, the shrill sound shattered the stillness in the office, and Sean moved back. Her hands rested on his chest, and the flush in her cheeks made her coloring spectacular. If this call wasn't life-and-death, Mac knew, he'd want the caller drawn and quartered.

The instant he kissed her, wild ideas of making use of that blanket came into his mind. Ideas of Sean coming to him, her body under his hands, her eyes filling with passion.

She looked up at him as the phone kept ringing. "The phone," she whispered, her voice as unsteady as he felt. "It might be important."

Not as important as what was happening in this room, he thought, but he didn't utter the words. Instead, he said, "Just a minute," and crossed to grab the receiver. "What is it?"

"An overseas call for you," Meg said. "From the Paris office."

Mac didn't know much about the time difference between Seattle and Paris, but he guessed it had to be at least half a day. That made it well after working hours in Paris. "Who is it?"

"A Mr. Dupont."

He'd completely forgotten about the man calling before. "Can you have him call back in a while?"

"Sir, he's called three times while you were having lunch, and I know you said you didn't want to be disturbed, but he's very insistent."

Mac held up one finger to Sean, who nodded, then turned and wandered over to what was left of the picnic. As she bent and reached for the bouquet of roses on the chest, he said, "Okay, put him on," not taking his eyes off Sean.

The line clicked. Then: "Charles?"

He watched Sean hold the arrangement and finger the velvety petals of one of the flowers. "Yes, what can I do for you?"

"Well, it's about time. I was getting the idea that you didn't want to talk to me."

"It's late there, isn't it?"

"Yes, it's late. That doesn't matter."

"Okay, we're talking. What do you want?" he said with an edge in his tone.

"I want to know what's going on. It can't be taking you this long to figure out if everything's a go. I just need the word from you."

Sean had put the roses on the floor and gathered up the dishes and the leftover food and put them in the basket. As she walked to the windows, Mac saw the noontime sun surrounding her, making her hair into a halo. "I need a bit more time," he said, not knowing what the man was talking about.

"Damn it," the man bit out, and his anger jarred Mac. "You aren't changing your mind are you?"

"Why would I?"

"Why wouldn't you?"

"No reason to."

"You'd better be damn sure that there isn't a reason."

"I can't talk right now, but we'll iron this out later."

"Just tell me how much longer you think it's going to take to confirm things."

"I'll let you know."

"When?"

Mac closed his eyes, nerves beginning to bunch at the base of his neck. "When *I* know." Puzzles and riddles. He hated it. "That's as specific as I can be right now."

"Hey, I'm getting strange signals from you, and I don't like it."

Mac wished he could say something to calm this man down, and he wished he knew why an employee would talk to him like this. But Charles might not even have been in charge. What if he had put this man in charge, then taken off to do his own thing? No matter what, Charles Elliot was still in charge. "I don't have time for this right now."

"You'd better make time," the man said. "I'm not going to let you give me the runaround. I thought you understood that before you left."

"I understand," Mac said. "And I'll be in touch." As he hung up, he heard the man say something else, but it was cut off as the receiver hit the cradle.

He knew he'd have to face the business side of Charles Elliot's life sooner or later, the problems he'd left behind from his life in Paris. He'd need to clear up loose ends like Paul Dupont. But right now he had his hands full with his life here. "Sean?"

She turned and silently walked back to where he stood. A frown tugged at her finely arched eyebrows. "You look worried. Was that something about the missing money?"

"No. Just Dupont again. He's overreacting to some business. I should have told him he could have my old job. That would have made things better, I suppose."

"Would you really let him have it?"

He looked into her eyes. "He's welcome to it."

She smiled. It was a gentle lifting of her lips that made a glow deep in her eyes. "I can't believe you're saying that."

He touched her cheek. "Believe it."

She covered his hand with hers and pressed her cheek against his open palm. "I really need to get back to work."

"I know. This date's over."

"Thanks for everything."

"Thanks for giving me another chance," he said.

Her smile faltered, and when she spoke again, her words were unsteady. "A second chance. Not many people get that, do they?"

He knew that better than anyone. He had his second chance, and he wasn't going to blow it. "No, they don't." He touched his lips to her forehead, relishing the warmth of the connection. Then he drew back and looked down at her. "Let's make the most of it."

"You've got a deal," she murmured.

"A promise."

She nodded. "A promise." Then she turned and quietly left the room. No sooner had the door closed than there was a soft knock on it, and Mac hurried across to pull it open. When he saw Meg there, he felt a degree of disappointment that Sean hadn't come back. "Yes?"

"Do you want me to take the picnic things out?"

"Yes, thanks," he said as he stood back.

She stepped inside to the picnic area. "I got you on-line with the computer in the accounting department, and you've got open access to all the company files that were initiated at any office in the past two years." She reached for the wicker basket. "Did you need anything else?"

"Do you know if I left any personal things here when I transferred to the Paris office?"

"I've only been here a year, but I don't think anyone else has used this office." She reached for the roses. "What do you want to do with these?"

He crossed and took them from her. "I'll keep them here." He went to the desk and put them down by the phone.

"Anything else?" Meg asked.

He turned to her. "No, thanks."

She picked up the blanket and the basket, then crossed to the door.

"No calls unless they're from my wife or Mr. Warren," he said. "If Mr. Dupont calls, tell him I'm busy."

"Yes, sir," she said, and left, closing the door behind her.

Mac stood in an emptiness that seemed palpable now that Sean had left. Then, with a glance at the roses, he went to his desk and sat in the wing-backed leather chair. He went through the drawers one by one, until he tried the last one on the bottom. It was the only one that was locked, and it only took him a minute to jimmy the lock with a heavy paper clip. When he slid the drawer open, he found it empty except for an old shoe box held shut by two heavy rubber bands.

Chapter Ten

Mac lifted the box out of the drawer, put it on the desk and slid the bands off. As he lifted the lid, he found a collection of photos held together by a frayed string. They were wedged against the side of the box by a stack of six or seven envelopes. Taking up the rest of the space were two books, a watch with a broken strap, and some pens and pencils.

Mac took out the pictures and sorted through the twenty or so odd-sized snapshots, which were yellowed with age. From the notations on the backs of them, Mac could trace Charles Elliot from a toddler with large eyes and torn pants to a teenager with a sullen expression, cropped hair and bare feet.

Only one picture was different. It was of two adults who looked like blue-collar workers. On the back was the notation Vera and Chuck at the house. The man, in a work shirt and overalls, had the same expression as the young Charles, almost sullen, and the plump, dark-haired woman, in a loose housedress, was staring at her feet. Charles Elliot's parents.

From the pictures, Mac could see that Charles came from poverty. He wondered if the contents of the envelopes would complete the picture. They were letters from someone named Sid Evans, writing to Charles while he was in college in Chicago. The writer was someone Charles had known when he was younger. The man was impressed that Charles had his life so well planned out. The writer admired Charles's plan to get everything he wanted, and never to have to worry about money again.

The books were college textbooks on finance, and the watch had a broken link in its expansion band. It had stopped at twelve o'clock.

As Mac repacked the box, he knew that his physical resemblance to Charles Elliot wasn't their only common ground. Charles had been mercenary in his search for a wealthy existence that he thought would banish his poor youth. Mac had been mercenary about finding a new life that would banish a past as empty as a black hole.

When Mac put the box back and closed the drawer, he sat back in his chair. Two men, two goals. Selfish goals. His phone rang, and he reached for it. "Yes?"

"Sir, I know what you said, but Mr. Dupont's been calling again. This is the third time."

Mac raked his fingers through his hair and exhaled. "Tell him I'm gone for the day." He glanced at the computer. "Meg, can you tell me how to get into the personnel files for the company?"

"Shift-F8."

He hit the keys, but all that came up on the screen was a flashing yellow strip that read "Enter password."

"Do you know the password, Meg?"

"No, sir. Not for those files."

"Who would?"

"Your wife."

"Connect me with her office, please."

"Yes, sir."

There was a silence, and then Meg was back on the line. "She's not answering, sir."

"Leave a message for her to call me when she gets back to her office, please."

"Yes, sir."

Mac put down the phone, and had barely turned back to the computer when the door swung open. Sean was in the entry, a paper in her hand. The anger in her expression was thunderous.

She threw the paper on the desk and glared at him. "Enough is enough, Charles! I knew this whole new image was a crock!"

He'd reached for the paper, but didn't look at it. "Tell me what's going on."

She took a deep breath, then folded her arms over her breasts. "You told Barret that you were leaving him alone, that you wouldn't do anything to take his land."

"I meant it."

"Sure. That's why this was faxed to you last Friday, with orders to hold it and you'd be in to get it. They gave it to me by mistake."

He looked down at the paper and skimmed the letter, which was printed under the logo of a law firm. The essence was that he could challenge Barret's right to the land under a seldom-used deed program that dated back to the thirties. Charles hadn't pulled any punches. Mac looked up at Sean, hating the anger that burned in her eyes. "I'm sorry."

"Sorry? You're not going to take his land!"

"That's right."

She faltered. "But, that letter—"

"Is a part of the past." He rang for Meg and when she looked in, he held out the paper to her. "Meg, would you please send a letter to this firm and tell them to drop all proceedings regarding this land?"

Meg came to take the letter. "I'll get on it as soon as I can."

Mac didn't take his eyes off Meg. "I'd appreciate it if you'd do it right now. I want it out within the hour."

"Yes, sir," Meg said, and quickly left.

When the door shut, Mac said, "I really am sorry. I forgot about that, otherwise I would have canceled it myself."

High color still dotted her cheeks, making the rest of her skin look like alabaster, and her lashes swept low over her eyes. "I'm the one who's sorry," she murmured. "I should have checked first before getting upset."

"You had every right to get upset." Charles had primed her to expect the worst. That would change. "But I'm glad you're here, actually."

"Why?"

Because I like looking at you, he wanted to say, but he actually said, "I need to know the password for the personnel files in the computer."

She didn't hesitate before giving it to him, and that made him feel as if he had just crossed some invisible hurdle with her. "It's LINK. If you need any other passwords, just let me know."

"Have you found anything yet?"

"No. I've got a meeting with Louis and Quint at five to discuss things."

"Good. I'll be there. Where is it?"

"In the chamber," she said, without giving him any idea about what "the chamber" might be.

"Is the Barret thing settled?" he asked.

She shrugged, the movement touched by a certain degree of nervousness. "Yes, I think it is."

"Good."

"We can leave after the meeting to go home and make the six-o'clock ferry. Is that okay with you?"

"That's fine."

"I'll let you get back to work."

"You, too."

She hesitated, then turned and quietly left.

Mac sank back in the chair as the door closed behind Sean, and he wondered what other surprises Charles had in store for him. Whatever they were, he just hoped he could clear them up as quickly as he had this one.

And he was starting to fit in. He'd arranged to sit in on the meeting, and then he'd be going back to the island with Sean. He needed to see a bit more of Louis to figure out where the man was coming from, and then he was going home with his wife. It felt right.

He looked at the computer, then sat forward to type in the password. The next thing that appeared on the screen was a directory of all the branches of Warren International. As he went through the directories, he began to hum the song he and Sean had danced to at the party.

He highlighted the directory for the Paris office, and once he opened it he found Paul Dupont's name and went into the man's personnel file. He'd hired on three years ago as an accountant at the office. He was fifty-one, single, from New York, fluent in French and German, and he'd started out at a salary that was probably twenty times more than Mac had ever made in any given year.

Even so, three months ago the man had received an impressive raise and the title Chief Accountant. There wasn't a clue to why he'd be so persistent calling Charles. Mac closed the file, then saw the one right below Dupont's. Charles James Elliot. He opened it and found out just what he'd known before about his educational background. Two addresses were given, the first in Paris, the second on the island. In the slot for the nearest relative not living with the employee, the word *none* was inserted. Then he saw the salary and let out a low whistle.

The man certainly hadn't been in danger of poverty, making money like that.

After he closed the files, he stared at the flashing prompt on the screen, then, on impulse, ran a general directory check. He scrolled down the screen, not quite sure what he was looking for. One directory was simply labeled CJE. Charles James Elliot? Mac typed it in, hit the Enter key and watched the screen go blank, then come up with a flashing Enter password prompt.

He sank back in the chair. He couldn't ask Sean for this password, not when in all likelihood it was Charles Elliot's own personal file. He had to do this on his own. He typed in LINK, but it didn't work. Then he tried random names, places, even the island's name. But nothing unlocked it. He searched through the desk for a book or sheet of paper with passwords. Then he put the briefcase on the desk and opened it.

He'd looked through it at the house and found company papers, some bills. There wasn't anything in it that helped. As he went to close it, he saw an almost hidden slit along the right side. He ran his fingers over the lining and felt a slight bulge. Finding an opening, he reached in and took out a red envelope that he saw was the folder for an airline ticket.

He opened it and found a one-way ticket in the name of Sidney Evans, first class, nonstop to Geneva. The date was just over a week away. Sidney Evans? Charles's college friend? The ringing of the phone startled him, and he reached for the receiver. "Yes?"

"Charles? Are you coming in for the meeting?" Sean asked.

He glanced at the clock. Five minutes to five. He quickly pushed the ticket back into the side slot. "Sure. Would you come by here, and we'll go in together?"

"I'm on my way."

Mac put the phone receiver back in the cradle, then snapped his briefcase shut. He'd check on the ticket as soon as he could. Taking the briefcase with him, he headed for the door and left the office to meet Sean and have her lead the way to "the chamber."

An hour later, when Mac and Sean finally left the meeting, Mac didn't know much more than he had when he went in. Except that "the chamber" was Louis Warren's private office, a space decorated to look like an English pub, with dark wood and brass, and a feeling that the man had been there forever.

Louis had seemed surprised to see Mac there, but he'd included him in all the conversations with Orin Quint, the accountant. The feeling that Louis was just waiting to catch Mac in a slipup wasn't there this time. And Mac began to wonder if he'd imagined it.

Settled in the car next to Sean as she drove through the early-evening streets of Seattle, heading for the ferry landing, Mac could see her nervousness in the way she gripped the wheel.

"Quint wasn't much help, was he?" he asked.

"No, he wasn't. I thought he could just go through the books, and even if it took a week he could pinpoint the leak. But he can't."

"At least he has an exact figure," Mac murmured as he shifted to rest his shoulder against the door and watch Sean. "Two million five hundred thousand dollars and no cents."

"That doesn't help."

He could see the tension in her jaw and shoulders. He had the most incredible desire to help her. He hadn't ever suspected that he had a touch of the protector in him. Walking away from the jail in New Orleans had been so simple. Just leave. Just walk out. It hadn't mattered to him who went to jail or who was freed. But this woman made him want to slay dragons and work miracles.

"You don't suppose that Quint has some part in this, do you?" The man had made him uneasy, and he wasn't sure if it was because he was such a computer nerd, or because he was so edgy.

Sean considered the question for a moment, then shook her head. "No, I don't think so. He's been with us for a long time, and he's always done a stellar job."

"Maybe he got tired of a weekly paycheck and decided to take early retirement."

She cast him a look touched with a frown. "What are you trying to tell me?"

"Nothing. I just never trusted anyone to be perfect forever. God knows, most people are less than perfect. Even the good ones."

"That sounds cynical," she murmured.

"It's realistic. People are seldom what they seem."

She slowed as she came to the street that ran parallel to the water. "I guess you're right. A few days ago I would never have thought you'd willingly be at work here or sitting in on a meeting like that."

And he couldn't believe how close he had come to his own truth. "Does Helen leave before you get home?"

"Usually I'm home by six." She glanced at the clock in the car. "Since we're not going to make the ferry until six-thirty, she probably left something for dinner and went on home."

As Sean slipped down the ramp to the waiting area for the ferry, Mac glanced at the briefcase at his feet. "Does Warren International have an office in Geneva?"

She shook her head as she braked to a stop. "No. Of course we don't. You know that."

He let that pass. "Have you ever been to Geneva?"

"No. Never." She shifted in the seat to look at him. "Have *you* been to Geneva?"

"No."

"Why the interest?"

"I was just wondering." He glanced at the ferry, which was just pulling to a stop. As the cars disembarked in a single file and drove past their car, he said, "Did you ever meet Sidney Evans?"

She shook her head. "Who is he?"

"Just someone I used to know." He sat back in the seat and tried to remember the address he'd seen on the envelopes in Charles's shoe box. Chicago. That was all he could remember.

Someone knocked on the window, and Sean pushed the button to lower it. A kid about twelve was there holding a paper out to her. "Fifty cents for an evening paper."

Sean took a couple of quarters out of the armrest and handed them to him, then took the paper. She handed it to Mac as she slowly inched the car onto the deck of the ferry. "What are you going to do this evening?" she asked.

Mac glanced down at the paper in his lap, and as he turned it over he saw an item in the lower left corner. *Hit and run victim identified.* He scanned the single column of text and felt his stomach tighten.

The victim of a hit and run accident outside the Belly Up Bar and Grill near the docks has been identified as Mackenzie Gerard, 36. Gerard's last known address was on the East Coast, and no relatives have been found. The police are still looking for a man Gerard met in the bar, who they believe witnessed the hit and run.

"Charles?"

When Sean touched his arm, Mac dropped the paper. Quickly he folded it over to cover the story and looked at Sean. "I'm sorry."

"I was asking what you're going to do this evening."

He was surprised to see that they were almost to Sanctuary Island. He hadn't even been aware of leaving the dock in Seattle. He pressed his hand to the paper, then closed his eyes. His own obituary. The thought ran a chill up his spine. Mackenzie Gerard was really dead.

"I'm tired. I think I need to get to bed early."

"Is your head bothering you?"

He felt the ferry begin to stop, its motors reversing, then the thump of the hull sliding into the piling channel. "A bit. Maybe I overdid it today."

The car started, and he felt it creeping off the ferry and onto the incline to the landing. "Are you going in to the office tomorrow?"

"Yes." He pressed the bridge of his nose between his thumb and forefinger. "I'll be ready to leave when you are."

MAC STOOD ON THE TERRACE in the silence of the night, staring out at the Sound and at the lights of Seattle in the distance. He'd hated staying away from Sean since they got back to the house, but the sight of his own obituary in the paper had brought all the lies into focus, all the lies he'd have to live with until the end of his life if he stayed here as Charles Elliot.

A part of him had known that was the way it would be. It couldn't have been any different. But he still hated the lies.

He felt the balmy breeze of the night travel across the lawn, the freshness of grass and water mingling sweetly in the air. He'd thought that once he had

Charles Elliot's life for his own he'd feel free. He'd thought he'd have an existence that would give him everything he'd never had before. What he had was a handful of lies and a growing need for a woman who didn't even know who he was.

When he sensed Sean behind him, he pushed his hands in the pockets of his slacks and balled them into fists. When she spoke, his hands tightened until his nails dug into his palms.

"I didn't know you were still up," she said. He felt her arm brush his, and he could inhale her sweetness along with the night fragrances. "It's beautiful out here, isn't it?"

He stared at the glow of Seattle in the distance until it blurred. When her hand touched his arm, he held his breath.

"Charles, what's wrong?"

He shook his head, wishing she wouldn't touch him. "I was just thinking about things."

"What?"

"Life. This place. The company."

"That covers just about everything," she said as her fingers moved on his arm, their warmth gentle and compelling. "Almost."

"What else is there?" he asked.

Her touch stilled on him, then was gone. A sense of isolation ate at him. "Us."

He closed his eyes for a long moment. "Is there an us?"

"I would have said no until this afternoon, but now I think there might be. Or could be." She moved even closer. "If you meant what you said about starting over again. If it's not all just lies."

He opened his eyes to the night. "I meant it. I just don't know if it's possible."

She moved to come around and stand in front of him. "How do you know unless we try?" she whispered.

He looked down at her. Her beauty was so much more than just physical. And, lacking the will to fight it, he acted on his impulse and reached out for her. He touched her cheek, then trailed his fingers to her lips. And the ache in him that had been there since the first time he saw this woman grew into an exquisite agony of need.

"God, you're beautiful," he breathed.

She laid her hands on his chest and parted her lips. Her moist heat touched the tips of his fingers as she found the buttons on his shirt with her hands. Slowly, as she drew gently on his fingers, she undid the buttons on his shirt, then pushed the silky material aside.

He gasped as her hands found his bare chest, then his nipples, which hardened at the contact. His gaze held hers, and as she played her tongue over his fingertips he thought he saw pleasure flicker in her eyes. Then she came closer, and as his hand moved to the nape of her neck, she pressed a scorching kiss on his bare chest.

"We...we agreed to go slowly," he said, his voice a low groan, as her mouth found his nipple and teased it with her tongue. "Sean, we..." His voice trailed off as she moved back just a bit, without breaking their contact.

"We have gone slowly," she whispered, then leaned up to touch her lips to his.

Mac knew he was lost the instant he tasted her. He knew there was no turning back, no way that he could deny what was going on between them. He wanted her, and even if he couldn't say it out loud, his body made no secret of his desire. He held her tight, his hips against hers, his mouth devouring hers, and the idea of being one with another human being finally made sense to him.

She trailed her lips to his throat, then to his exposed shoulder, and whispered against his skin, "I want you to make love to me."

Love. God help him, but he did love this woman. He loved her in a way he hadn't known existed until now. In three short days, he'd fallen head over heels in love. He buried his fingers in her silky hair, and he knew that the moment in the office the day of the party had been just a preliminary for this moment. For the inevitable.

He kissed her hair, her temples, and inhaled her scent. Then she moved back, just enough to meet his gaze, and he saw the desire he felt reflected in her eyes. "I didn't know it until today." Her hands slipped under his shirt to circle his waist and spread on his back. "I really love you, Charles."

Mac framed her face with both of his hands. She loved Charles. She loved a man who didn't exist anymore. He touched his lips to hers, then drew back. She didn't love Mackenzie Gerard. She didn't even know he existed. The idea made a sadness grip his heart, and all his need and desire centered in an incredible ache.

"I know," he whispered. "But I meant it about taking our time. I want this to be right when it happens . . . for both of us."

He could feel her tense, but she didn't move. "What do you mean?"

"It's been four years. For heaven's sake, I didn't even make our honeymoon. How do you know you can trust me now? How do you know it's right?"

"I know," she said simply, but the glow was gone from her eyes.

"No, you don't." He drew back. If he ever made love to Sean, it would be because she really loved him, the man behind the illusion. Not the lies and the false image. "Neither do I."

She backed up, her eyes wide. "That's it?"

He was doing this all wrong, but for a man who had never cared much about honor and decency in his life, those ideas suddenly felt like the cornerstone of his existence. He wouldn't take advantage of her vulnerability. He couldn't do that to her. "Sean, I just—"

She cut him off. "No, I won't do this again." She bit her lip hard, then exhaled. "I won't."

When he reached out to touch her face, she flinched away from the contact, and he hated himself almost as much as he hated the lies. All of his own making, drunk or sober. "I'm sorry."

"Don't be. I don't want pity." She swept her arms out to her sides. "I don't need this, the picnic where I thought just about anything was possible, then you proving you meant it about Barret's land, now this coldness. I won't ask for anything from you again."

With that she pushed past him, and he could hear her feet strike the stones of the terrace. The door closed with a cracking sound, and as he flinched at the noise he uttered a frustrated curse that shattered the night.

WHEN SEAN SAW CHARLES waiting for her the next morning, she forced herself to ignore him. She had begun to think she'd lost the ability to sleep at all. Between reliving the episodes with Charles, the ups and downs, the heat and the chill, and worrying about the business, she'd tossed and turned all night. She'd gone over and over things until she thought she'd go mad.

The business was in danger of falling apart, and she couldn't do a thing about it. And she felt about ready to fall apart around Charles. He'd wanted her last night. She'd felt it and known it, yet he'd stopped her dead in her tracks.

And she'd meant it about loving him, as astounding as that was to her, but even as the words had been uttered she'd seen him close down. Now the man watching her as if he were taking inventory showed no reaction. She just hoped she looked equally under control, even though the sight of him in a smartly tailored beige suit worn with a dark brown shirt and no tie was making her mouth go dry.

Damn it, she'd never been a simpering fool when it came to men. Not even when she'd decided to marry Charles. She'd felt as if it were the right thing to do, and she'd always thought that the very idea of melting at the sight of a man was utter nonsense. Now she wasn't so sure.

She nodded to Charles when she got to the bottom of the staircase, then brushed past him to head for the door. Hopefully he'd stay quiet on the way to the city and she could get herself settled for the day. But once they were in her car, her hopes were dashed on many counts.

"I need some information," he said as he got settled in the car.

"What?" The word was abrupt and almost harsh, but he didn't seem to notice or care.

"The passwords the company uses. Are they predetermined? If the files are for a certain office, a certain password is used?"

"No. Passwords are changed regularly, and only the people who need to know them know them." She gripped the wheel as she drove down toward the ferry dock. "Why do you ask?"

"I didn't remember how it worked," he said. Then she finally got her wish, as he sank into a silence that seemed almost tangible.

Sean concentrated on driving and tried to ignore the man so close to her. But by the time she was in Seattle, heading away from the waterfront, she knew how futile it was—almost as futile as trying to sleep had been last night.

"Are you going to say it?" he asked suddenly as the Warren building came into view.

She didn't look at him. "There isn't anything to say."

"Isn't there?"

As she swung the car into the parking garage and nodded to the attendant at the entrance, she said, "What would I have to say to you right now?"

"You can call me a bastard if you want. I deserve it."

She felt heat rising in her face. "It's not important right now."

"If you say so."

She pulled into her parking space and stopped the car, giving away her anger by the slight squeal of the tires on the concrete floor. Yanking the key out of the ignition, she turned on Charles. "Don't do that!"

"Do what?"

"Bait me like that. I'm not about to go over what happened last night. I told you I never would. One thing I thought you knew about me is that I don't lie. I don't make idle threats. I meant what I said."

"Then why the anger?"

To deny she was angry would have been foolish, so she turned away from him, gripped the door handle and got out. Without waiting for him, she headed for the elevators, reaching them just as one of the doors slid open. Stepping in, she turned, hoping that Charles wouldn't make it before the doors closed, but he was right behind her. He stepped inside with her and hit a button.

She stared at her reflection in the polished doors, and even she could see the anger that was evident in her mouth and eyes. She looked awful, as if she hadn't slept in a week. Her life was in the toilet, and this man was making her so angry she could barely see straight.

She closed her eyes, but then, after quietly counting to ten, she opened them again and made herself look at Charles. His blue eyes were on her, and as the elevator stopped at their floor and the doors began to open, she muttered, "You *are* a bastard," then turned and walked out.

Chapter Eleven

Mac didn't attempt to contact Sean all morning. He sat alone in his office and went over all the papers Charles had in his office, trying to find the password to open the CJE file. But by eleven o'clock he was no closer to seeing the contents of the file than he had been when he started.

When Meg knocked on the door and came into his office, he was thankful for the interruption. "Mr. Elliot, your wife told me to tell you that she's lunching with her father."

"Did she say anything else?"

"She said to tell you that she'll be here until six, and if you want to you can take a company car to the island earlier."

"Oh, did she?"

"Yes, sir."

"Tell her I'll be ready to go home at six...with her."

She nodded, then ducked back out.

Mac sat back in his chair, mulling over his last words to Meg. He'd go home with Sean at six. It *was* home to him. He'd just have to figure out how to deal with his newly minted conscience—and the woman he loved.

But right now he wanted to get into Charles Elliot's private files. He sat forward and reached for the briefcase, opened it and took out the airline ticket. Sidney Evans. He got out the shoe box again, looked at the return address on one of the envelopes, then called directory assistance in Chicago.

He got the phone numbers for six Sidney Evanses who lived in the area. One by one he called them, introducing himself as Charles Elliot and waiting for a reaction. When the fourth number was answered by a woman, he went through his routine.

"Hello. This is Charles Elliot calling."

But this time, when he said his name, there wasn't a blank silence on the other end, then a "Who?" This time the woman said, "Charles, how nice of you to call again."

"Nice to talk to you again, too."

The woman spoke in a low voice. "I was surprised to hear from you the first time, six months ago. I told you when my Sidney died five years ago, I tried to find you, since you were his friend back in college. I was relieved when I could finally let you know. My son never forgot you. He always said you'd be someone some day."

So, Sidney Evans was dead. "I appreciate that, Mrs. Evans."

"Did you have any luck getting the information you were asking for?"

"Information?"

"You know, Sidney's death notices. I never thought to keep the write-up in the paper's obituary column or anything. Sort of morbid, you know."

"I understand. I just wanted to call and see how you're doing."

"I'm doing all right."

"Good."

"I thank you for inquiring."

"Thank you, and take care." He hung up and sat back in his chair. When Charles had bought that ticket, he'd known Sidney was dead, and had been for five years. He could use that name without any problem. He could probably even use his social security number and get a passport in that name. But why?

He dialed the number on the airline ticket folder to confirm the flight to Geneva, Switzerland. When it was confirmed, he asked, "Could you tell me what credit card I used to pay for it? I didn't keep track, and I need to know for my records."

She was silent for a moment, then said, "It shows here that the ticket was paid with cash at our Paris office."

"Thanks," he murmured, and hung up.

He stared at the ticket in his hand. A ticket for a dead man. Then he looked at the computer. Quickly he tried to pull up the CJE file and when the password prompt flashed, he typed in Evans, but nothing happened. Then he typed Sidney Evans. The screen went blank, then filled with a financial record that he knew had nothing to do with the Warren company.

Mac didn't know a great deal about electronic banking, but as he read the documents in the file he knew he'd found the money that was missing from the company. Charles Elliot had funneled it off into a bank account in Geneva, Switzerland. When he got to the bottom of the file, he found the total of the deposits in the account. Two million, five hundred thousand dollars.

He had grown tired of waiting to get money in bits and pieces through Sean and her father. He hadn't been about to divorce Sean and get a settlement that might have lasted him a few years if he lived well. The man had wanted money, and he'd wanted it immediately.

He sank back in the chair. Charles had milked the money from the company and had been prepared to disappear. The idea didn't shock Mac, but it left a bitter taste in his mouth. Charles hadn't been coming home last Friday. He must have been coming back to clear up any evidence, in the hope that no one would even know what had happened until after he dropped out of sight.

The irony of Charles Elliot taking over a dead man's name to make a new life for himself wasn't lost on Mac. There was a black humor to it. Very black. The man had planned to leave Sean and Louis holding the bag. It wouldn't have bothered him a bit. Hurting people just didn't seem to have mattered to the man.

It hadn't taken long to find that Charles was a loser, despite his appearance. He'd been a grasping person intent on getting his share, a man who hadn't even known the gem he had in his own wife. But taking the name Charles Elliot meant taking on his past.

Mac hit the arm of the chair, then sat forward. At least Charles hadn't pulled it off. The money was still sitting in the bank in Geneva, and if it had been transferred there quietly, it could be transferred back. He looked at the clock. Almost noon. He had six hours until he was going to leave with Sean.

With any luck at all, he could have everything fixed by the time he went back to Sanctuary Island. And he knew that when he did he was going to tell Sean everything, about the money, about the plans Charles had made, and, most importantly, about Mac Gerard. He'd take whatever came. He just wanted out of the lies.

For the rest of the day, through trial and error, Mac managed to get the money out of the bank in Geneva and into the main account at Warren International. When he finally erased the CJE files and closed the computer down, it was almost five-thirty.

He picked up the phone and asked Meg to get Sean for him. "She left an hour ago. She said you could take that company car, or you could stay in the city for the evening. It was up to you."

"Do you know if she went straight home?"

"I believe she did."

"Then please get me a company car as quickly as you can."

"I'll have one brought to the side entrance in five minutes," she said, then hung up.

SEAN WASN'T IN ANY MOOD to make small talk with Charles or be close to him in the confines of her car. Her nerves were raw, and she needed space and time alone to try and figure out what was going on. She didn't want to sense his nearness, to inhale his scent and know there was something going on. Something she didn't understand. And she knew it wasn't that he wanted to take their relationship slowly. After last night, she didn't buy that at all.

The idea that he was manipulating her was weighing heavily on her, and by the time she drove off the ferry and onto the island she had a terrible headache. She had given Charles the last of the aspirin and she needed some. Instead of heading for the house, she turned toward the only real town on Sanctuary Island. Fontaine was three miles inland from her place.

Minutes later, she drove onto Main Street, an area maybe ten blocks long, with small businesses and houses lining the way under ancient trees. When she pulled into the parking area for the market, there was only one other car there. She recognized Jerry Potts, the kid who had helped with the Fourth of July party.

He was in an old gray pickup with two other men about his age, and she could see cans of beer lying on the ground, as if they'd been dropped out the window. She nodded to him when he called out to her, then went into the store and bought some aspirin. When she came out, thankfully, the parking lot was empty.

She got into her car, pulled out onto Main Street and headed home. She passed the ferry landing just as the ferry was approaching the landing area, and she headed up the road to the top of the bluffs. But partway up she felt the car hesitate, then sputter. One glance at the gas gauge and she knew what was wrong.

She was below empty. As the car died, she coasted to the side of the road and stopped. She looked ahead at the winding road shaded by large firs and evergreens, their shadows long in the early-evening light. It wasn't raining, and she wasn't more than half a mile from her house. She wasn't going to just sit here letting her frustration grow. The cellular phone wouldn't work this close to the bluffs. Maybe the walk would do her good.

She pushed her purse under the seat, took the keys out of the ignition and opened the door. As she stepped out onto the blacktopped road and locked the door, she heard an engine, coming closer.

At first she thought all her attempts to get away from Charles had been dashed, and he was coming up the hill. But as she turned to look back down the road, she saw the gray pickup from town coming up the hill. Jerry was driving, and the other two were in the bed of the truck. They were swaying and bracing themselves on the cab. They all had open beer cans.

The truck pulled in behind her car at a skewed angle, and then the engine died. While the two men jumped down from the bed of the truck, Jerry got out of the cab. Sean could tell they were all drunk. Jerry steadied himself with one hand on the door of the truck and tossed an empty beer can over the cab and into the brush on the side of the road.

"Looks like you've got car trouble," he said, in an overly loud voice that was slurred from the alcohol.

The other two were larger than Jerry, and looked as if they might be brothers. One downed the last of his beer, crushed the can in his hand, then threw it back over his head. It clattered down the hill on the road. The other man rested one arm on Jerry's shoulder and leered at Sean. "So, you got car trouble, and we're good Samaritans," he said.

The other two laughed as if he'd said the funniest thing they'd ever heard. Sean knew she was in trouble. She considered locking herself inside the car, but she knew that by the time she got the key in the lock and managed to open the door, all three of them could be right by her.

She looked up and down the road, but there wasn't another car in sight. She was isolated, and she knew her only option was to bluff her way along and hope they were simply drunk and not dangerous.

"Boy, I'm glad you came along. I've run out of gas, and I would appreciate it if you could get me some."

"You need something to get your engine started?" the man leaning on Jerry's shoulder said.

"I need a gallon of gas," she said, keeping her voice even and hoping the fear that was starting to nudge at her wouldn't be evident to them.

Jerry reached back into the truck and took out a six-pack with two cans missing, then started toward her, with the other two men right behind him. "Make you a deal," he said as he came closer. "I'll get your engine going, since you sure as hell get mine going." Any hope that she could talk her way out of this died when Jerry came within a few feet of Sean and the other two men surrounded her.

Sean gripped the key in her hand so tightly it cut into her skin. "Please, I'll just walk home. I can get gas there."

Someone touched her shoulder, and she held her breath as he came close enough to talk into her ear. "We're going to party, and you're going to be our entertainment."

MAC FELT a certain sense of rightness, knowing that he had been the one to find the money, and that he could go to Sean and tell her everything was all right. He drove up and off the ferry at six and through the parking area. With a right turn at the road, he started up the grade to the bluffs. As he rounded a turn partway up, he slowed.

It looked as if an accident might have occurred. An old, battered gray pickup truck partially blocked the road, its nose aimed precariously in the direction of the bluffs. But as he got closer, he realized it had been parked that way. And in front of it was Sean's sedan.

Then he saw three rough-looking men by Sean's car, almost hiding Sean from his sight. He headed for them, going around the truck and stopping right in the middle of the road, about five feet from the group. He jammed on the brakes, and as they squealed, the men turned to look at him. Sean was absolutely still, but he could tell she was scared to death.

The need to protect her came in such a rush that it consumed him. He jumped out of the car, with the engine running, and went around the car to get as close as he could to Sean. The men turned, blocking her against the driver's side of the car.

As Mac got close to the group, he could smell beer and could see the blurred eyes and slack mouths of the men. Then he recognized the nearest one, the kid who had been helping at the Fourth of July party, Jerry Something-or-other. He hadn't liked him then. He made him sick now.

He stared right at Jerry as he stepped in front of him, but his mind was on Sean, standing just behind the man. Without taking his eyes off Jerry, he held out his hand to Sean. "Let's go, Sean."

She reached out to take his hand, but Jerry blocked the contact. "She's with us. We're helping," he said, his words slurring. He wiped at his mouth with a hand that held an open beer can. "Just helping the lady."

The guy to the right of Sean leaned forward, his hand on Jerry's shoulder. "Just keep going, Pops. We can handle this."

"Oh, can you?" Mac asked. The other two men had a rawboned largeness, but they were both so drunk that their reflexes had to be trashed.

"Kirk, this guy's her old man," Jerry said.

The one he'd called Kirk shrugged. "So what? We got here first, and there's you and me and Stan against one of him."

Mac could see Jerry weighing the options. Then Stan, the other man against the car, said, "Ain't no way he can take us on. He's old and all pretty in his rich man's suit." When Stan tossed his beer can over the car into the bushes and stood straight, Jerry seemed to take on an added belligerence and lose the sense to back down.

Mac had been in enough street brawls in his life to know that there were no rules. He wasn't going to wait for them to decide just what they were going to do. He'd decide for them.

Before they could do anything, he reached for Jerry. He grabbed a fistful of his shirt, jerked on it, and smashed him into Kirk. Jerry's head hit the man full in the face, and from the sharp sound of the impact and his moan, he knew Kirk's nose was broken.

While Kirk dropped to his knees in the road, Mac literally yanked Jerry off his feet just as Stan lunged forward. He threw Jerry at Stan, and the two men tangled together as they fell sideways against the back fender of Sean's car. Jerry slipped sideways and struck his face on the bumper, while Stan jerked back and tried to break his fall to the road with his outstretched arm.

Mac had enough time to hear Sean scream before he turned to see Kirk coming at him. With blood gushing from his nose, the drunk lunged forward. At the same time, Mac swung full-force at his face and struck him squarely in the jaw. Kirk seemed to freeze for a full second. Then, slowly, he toppled backward like a felled tree.

Pain shot from Mac's hand, through his forearm, into his elbow, then radiated into his shoulder and neck. He muttered an oath that did nothing to help the pain, but did make Jerry jump. As Mac shook the feeling from his hand, he looked up at Sean, and as soon as they made eye contact, she ran toward him. The next thing he knew, she was in his arms, hugging him so tightly that he could barely get his breath. With his injured hand at his side, he held her close with his other hand, carefully watching the three men behind her.

Jerry rolled onto his side and slowly made his way to his feet, using Sean's car as his support. Stan was already up, muttering profanities, but staggering in the direction of the truck. Kirk was spread-eagled on the road, out cold. "Get your friends and get out of here," Mac said to Jerry.

"You gonna call the cops?"

He felt Sean pull even closer to him. "Let's put it this way. I won't, but if you don't leave now, you'll wish I did when I get through with you."

Jerry was sober enough to know Mac meant every word he said, and he made his way over to Kirk. He grabbed at his friend, tugging him to his feet, then half carried, half helped, the groggy Kirk toward the truck.

"Didn't mean nothing," Jerry muttered as he went past Mac and Sean without even looking at them. "Nothing. Just trying to help."

"Sure," Mac said, his hand throbbing. "A regular knight in shining armor."

Mac watched them get into the truck. Jerry half lifted, half pushed, Kirk over into the bed. Then he pulled himself up into the cab, where Stan was sitting holding his face. The truck started, then backed up just a bit until it could make a U-turn back down the hill. In one last act of defiance, Stan put his hand out the window and made an obscene gesture at Mac.

"Creep," Mac muttered, then gently held Sean back to look down into her face. She was pale, but she didn't look as if she'd been hurt. "Are you all right? They didn't—"

"No, they'd just gotten here a few minutes before you came. I'm fine. I—ran out of gas, and they stopped, and..." She shivered. "They were so drunk, and..."

"Forget it. They're gone now," Mac murmured.

"I can't believe you got them to leave. You took care of them like something out of a movie."

"Sure, just call me Clint Eastwood," he muttered, then drew his right hand back and shook it. "They just don't tell you in the movies that when you hit someone in the face it feels as if you broke every bone in your hand."

She reached for his hand. "You broke your hand?" she gasped, gently cradling it in both of hers as she studied it.

"No, it's not broken. Just sore."

She looked up at him, her tawny eyes filled with concern. Mac realized that in the time of dragons and knights, Sean would have been the woman he would have slain any beast for without thinking twice about it. "You have to soak it in cool water or ice," she murmured. "Let's get to the house. My car's locked. We can get it later."

Mac let Sean get in the driver's seat while he went around and got in the passenger side of the company car. As she drove onto the road and headed up the hill, he held his bad hand with his good one and asked, "Why did you leave without me?"

She didn't look at him. "I needed to think. To sort things out."

"Mcg said you left a while ago."

"I went into Fontaine to get some aspirin." She stopped by the security gate and automatically opened it. As the gates slid silently back, she drove up the driveway. "I just never thought to check the gas gauge. I was thinking about other things."

"What things?" he asked as she drove the car up the driveway.

"A lot of things," she said cryptically. As she drove under the portico, she glanced at Mac. "I feel as if I've been bombarded since I found out about the missing money."

"I was going to—"

She cut off his words by getting out and closing her door. He watched her walk around the front of the car, and then he opened his door and stepped out. She reached the entry stairs, then hurried up them as he followed. Arriving at where she stood, he waited for her to unlock the door and open it.

He went in after her. "Helen?" she called, but her own voice echoed back to her. She looked at Mac. "I guess Helen's gone for the day. Come on upstairs and let me doctor your hand."

She headed for the stairs, then started up, her hand on the satiny banister. He remembered what she'd said about sliding down banisters, about knowing how it might end before beginning. And he knew that life was never like that. If he'd thought out what he was doing when the accident happened, he would never have met this woman or finally figured out what it was like to really love someone.

He caught up to her at the doors to her bedroom, and when she went inside, he slowed his pace. The last time he'd stood here with Sean, he'd felt his lies weighing heavily on him. He'd been afraid to touch her, in case she knew he was an impostor. Now he almost wanted that to happen, to have everything out in the open, to clear the air.

He stepped into the suite, and went through to the main area, which was in soft shadows with the drapes closed. As he stopped by the bed, Sean called out from the bath, "Did you break the skin on your hand?"

He looked at his hand. Only a vague redness at his knuckles showed the reason for the throbbing. "No."

She came back into the room with a wet towel and stopped in front of him to reach for his hand. "Here, put this on your hand. It's cool, and it should make it feel better.''

He smiled at her as she concentrated on wrapping the towel around his hand. ''I'm sorry you left without me.''

Her hands stilled on him, and then she looked up, her amber eyes intent under dark lashes. ''I told you, I had to think.''

''You never did say what you had to think about.''

She drew her hand back, and he grasped the towel to keep it from falling off his hand. But he didn't look away from Sean. ''Everything,'' she said. ''The company, priorities, you, me. Everything.''

''Did you come to any decisions about any of the above?''

She stepped out of her pumps, pushing them toward the bed with her foot. ''Yes, as a matter of fact I did.''

''And are you going to tell me what you decided?''

She stood very still, the room's shadows gentle on her. Slowly she reached up to take the pins out of her hair, then shook the silky veil and took a step toward Mac. ''I decided that taking it slowly is good for a lot of things in this life. And taking things slowly is probably the most prudent thing to do with a relationship. But sometimes a person has to wade into life and find out what's there.''

He'd done that plenty of times, and had usually regretted it. Until now. ''And?'' he whispered.

She came closer, then slowly touched his chest with her hands. ''When you found me with those drunks, you went right in.'' She was so close he could feel her hips brush his, and a reaction that he had no control over began to build. "I, for one, am tired of analyzing and thinking and looking for what's at the end of every action I take." She undid the two buttons on his jacket, then worked her hands under it until she could push it off his shoulders and down until it slipped off and fell to the floor.

He stared into her face, knowing he could stop this anytime he chose to. But he didn't want to. He wanted Sean with him, completely and totally. He wanted to explore her and know her the way a lover should. When she reached up to touch his chin with her lips, she whispered, "I said I wouldn't do this again, but I was wrong. I lied. I never in my life wanted anyone the way I want you right now."

Mac gently laced his fingers in her loose, silky hair, then tipped her head so that her lips were offered to him. Her tawny eyes were heavy with a desire that was building in him with the speed of an out-of-control fire. "I want you, Sean," he said in a hoarse voice.

They stood like that for a moment, each almost afraid to move, in case the other one walked away. But when Sean touched her tongue to her pale lips, Mac bent his head and tasted her. He had passed the point of no return.

She came to him with a single-mindedness that stunned him, and with a passion that echoed his own.

Sean felt Charles under her hands, his heat against hers, his tongue invading her mouth, and felt a joy that she'd never known before. Surely this was the start of their marriage, not chronologically, but in every other way. And as she opened her mouth in invitation to his, she knew that love came to people in the strangest ways. It certainly had to her.

She went closer, as close as she could be to another human being. All she knew was that she wanted to be part of him. She wanted to know this man in every possible way. Her hands found his belt buckle, and she fumbled with the leather and metal. Then he covered her hands with his, and in one easy motion the belt was undone and she had found the zipper and slid it down.

Charles moved back and stepped out of his pants and socks and shoes. He stood in front of her in white boxer shorts, like the day she found him in her bed, but this time there was no anger in her and no hangover for him. She could clearly see the way he strained against the restrictive cloth barrier, and she went to him.

As soon as she felt him under her hands, he gasped and pulled her toward him, unbuttoning and tugging aside her blouse and undoing her skirt. There was nothing slow and easy about this. They were in a frenzy of need. Clothes were abandoned and tossed aside until Sean stood in nothing but her bra and panties.

He looked at her through the shadows, then touched her shoulders, his fingers as unsteady as her heartbeat. It all seemed so new—like it was the first time she had ever felt his heat, and the first time his fingers had slipped her bra straps off her shoulders. The flimsy material dropped, and she awkwardly reached behind her to undo the clasp and toss the bra with the other clothes. It felt like the first time he had ever touched her.

Chapter Twelve

With a foot of space separating them, Sean realized Charles was staring at her, but her nakedness wasn't awkward or embarrassing in any way. She loved the caress of his eyes on her, and the way he tried to smile, his expression faltering. And it took her breath away when his hands touched her breasts. The nipples instantly hardened, and the low moan that escaped from her parted lips echoed around them.

Then, before she knew what was happening, Charles had her in his arms, lifting her high against his heart, and was taking her to the bed. As they sank onto the coolness of the spread, he stretched out alongside her, his hand at her hips, his fingers working their way under the elastic of her panties. She helped him disentangle her legs from it, and then it was gone, and her nakedness was complete.

She lay on the bed as Charles raised himself up on his elbow and looked down at her. His hands weren't touching her, but his eyes were on every inch of her. She felt her growing readiness to have him take her, to have him inside her, to know him in a way she never had before.

When she felt as if she would explode if he didn't touch her, she moved to him and closed her hands over his shorts. He was hard and ready, as ready as she was, and she tugged at the waistband. He shifted, and the shorts were gone in one movement, until nothing stood between them. When she touched him again, skin on skin, she felt him tense. His groan of need was all around her.

His hand stilled on her breast as she looked at him, wishing there was full light. But in the shadows they relied on touch, and her hands knew him in a way that filled her with a need that threatened to fragment her. She pressed her lips to his chest, and as Charles fell back into the bedspread, she tasted his skin, trailing her mouth down to his navel, then lower, and his hands caught her shoulders when she found his center.

"No," he groaned. "Please." And he pulled her up until his lips found hers and their tastes mingled together.

He skimmed one hand down her back, to her hips, and when he brushed her inner thigh she closed her eyes and threw her head back on the pillows. The feelings were so intense, the slight abrasiveness of his touch such an erotic delight, that she bit her lip until she was certain she could taste blood.

His fingers were feathery at first, and when she arched toward his touch he covered her, the heel of his hand against the core of her, slowly rotating it until she was certain she would die from the exquisite feelings that surrounded her yet radiated from the center of her soul.

Charles had never done this to her. He had never touched her beyond the surface, and as she cried out, she knew that the Charles she had known was a thing of the past.

When Sean was certain she couldn't take it any longer, that she was going to feel things that couldn't be comprehended or endured, he moved over her and braced himself with his hands on either side of her shoulders. She looked up into his face, and knew a love that defied all reason and sanity.

She lifted her hips to him, wanting him in her, and he moved to her, tested her with his strength, then entered her, slowly and exquisitely. She closed her eyes and gasped as she accepted him completely. He was deep in her, and still above her. She opened her eyes.

"I love you," he said without moving. "I want you to know that, no matter what happens."

She clasped his hips, holding him against her, almost afraid for the moment when he would begin to move. "I love you, too," she managed, her voice hoarse and unsteady.

"Do you?" His voice held a hint of something she didn't understand, but then it was gone as he slowly began to stir inside her. She felt his full length ease in and out, and then he moved faster and faster. The feelings within her were building at a speed that was breathtaking. When she was certain she couldn't take it anymore, he plunged deep inside her, and the moment of complete freedom exploded in her.

She felt as if she had been taken out of this world and into another where it was just the two of them. Just a moment of rare and beautiful completeness. She had never been in that place before. Never. As she dissolved into sensations that shattered her, yet solidified her love for him, she knew she had never been with this man before.

MAC HELD SEAN TO HIS SIDE in the softness of the bedroom, relishing the way her legs lay heavily over his, the way her hand rested on his stomach. Whatever happened, he knew, this moment would be his forever. When he told her the full truth, if she turned from him, he would have the memory of a passion and a oneness that were unique, and truly the best thing that had ever happened in his life.

He felt her sigh as she snuggled into his shoulder, and he held her more tightly as he pressed a kiss to her hair. He trailed his fingers along her arm, feeling her smoothness under the roughness of his fingers. She felt like fine silk, and he wanted to lose himself in her again and again.

When her hand spread on his stomach, he knew she was awake, and he almost dreaded the thought of moving enough to make eye contact. Even with the shadows gathering in the room, he didn't want to see the truth there...not just yet. But as she shifted until she was raised up on her elbow, studying him through the shadows, he found himself holding his breath.

Her hand moved on him, trailing lower, to his navel, then stilled when he shuddered at the contact. "Sean...we need to talk."

She moved close to hush him with her lips on his, and her words made her breath mingle with his. "No, no talking. Not yet. Later. When this all makes sense." She touched her lips to the corner of his mouth, then slowly trailed them down to his ear, touching fire to his skin with each contact.

He closed his eyes, trying to control the spontaneous reaction of his body to her touch. Just a light touch, a gentle contact, and even though he was sated from the last time, he wanted more. He rolled onto his side, facing her in the shadows, and cupped his hand on her hip. As his mouth found hers, he invaded her warmth with his tongue, and drank deeply of an essence that was uniquely and beautifully hers.

When his hand moved to her waist, then to her breast, she arched toward him. With her head thrust back and her throat was exposed, he tasted the elegant sweep of her neck, while his hands cupped and teased her breasts until the nipples were hard nubs. Her legs wrapped around his, and her hips pushed against his desire. As her hand found his core, the hunger that he'd experienced the first time returned, but more powerful and more consuming than ever.

He turned, his hands spanning her waist, and lifted her over him. Slowly he entered her, the fit as perfect as if they had been created for each other. When she began to move, he cupped her hips and made her still for a moment. The feelings were so intense that they were almost painful, and he opened his eyes to see her leaning over him.

Her hair fell forward, a silky veil framing her beautiful face. Her lips were parted, her eyes were heavy with desire, and she was simply waiting. As he absorbed the sensation of the velvet heat that surrounded him, he eased the grip of his hands on her hips. Slowly, ever so slowly, she began to move again, and as the sensations built in him, he heard her say,

"It's you I want," and then everything was lost in the shattering ecstasy that seemed to take over his soul.

A few moments later—or perhaps it was an eternity—Mac had Sean next to him again, their heat and dampness mingling. He could feel her breathing returning to normal, just the way his was. Then echoing through the house, he heard chimes, like something out of Westminster Abbey. Sean stirred, raising on one elbow, and frowned at him. "I forgot to close the gate, didn't I?"

"We both did."

"Well, were you expecting anyone?"

"No. No one. You?"

"No." When the chimes sounded again, followed by a hollow pounding sound, she moved away from him. His skin felt cool as soon as she was gone, and he got up himself as she stood by the bed and reached for a robe lying on the footboard. "I'll check and see who it is."

Mac moved quickly, grabbing his slacks and putting them on. "No, don't. It could be those jerks again. They could have gone off drinking and come back for a confrontation."

She watched him as he zipped the slacks, then went with him toward the door. "Somehow, I think you'll take care of them."

He glanced at her, warmed by the comfortable smile on her face. "I'll do my best," he said, then moved ahead of her as the chimes sounded again and again, interrupted only by the pounding on the doors.

Sean followed her husband down the stairs and stopped at the last step as he strode toward the doors. His skin still held the sheen of moisture from their lovemaking, and his hair was mussed from her touch. She ran her tongue over her lips, a bit disappointed to find the taste of him had faded.

He opened the door and stood very still, staring at a thin man in a rumpled suit standing on the porch. The stranger was so blonde that his eyelashes and eyebrows weren't visible, and his thinning hair showed the pinkness of his scalp. He looked exhausted and flushed with anger.

As he looked into the house, the anger faltered, giving way to a flash of confusion. His hand, which was raised in a fist, as if to strike the door again, slowly lowered.

"What's going on?"

The stranger seemed unable to speak for a moment, but then he said, "Is this the Elliot house?"

"It is. Who are you?"

"Who are you?" he countered.

"I'm Charles Elliot."

His face flushed even more. "Like hell you are."

Sean held the banister as the two men faced each other. She knew somehow that life was about to alter completely for the two of them. Then Charles asked, "Who are *you?*"

"Paul Dupont, and I want to see Charles Elliot right now."

"You're looking at him." The voice, so even, so controlled, only infuriated the man more.

Paul Dupont pushed his way into the house, then stopped when he saw Sean on the stairs. "Mrs. Elliot?"

"Yes?" she said.

He nodded. "I'm sorry for this intrusion, but I need to talk to your husband."

She looked at Charles, who was still in the open doorway, staring at Paul Dupont. She saw him with such clarity that it almost made her eyes hurt. He was the man she had just made love with, and he was staring at the intruder with an expression that was totally unreadable. "This man is my husband."

Dupont narrowed his eyes, then said, "I don't know who this is, but he's not the same Charles Elliot who left Paris last Friday."

Sean heard his words as she looked at the man in the door. He wasn't Charles? She stared at him, gripping the banister so tightly that her fingers ached. "What are you—?"

"I came all the way from Paris to see Charles Elliot. I don't know what's going on here, but I won't be put off."

Sean couldn't take her eyes off the man behind Dupont. When his blue eyes met hers, the impact was stunning. For a moment she saw raw fear there, but then it was covered by a control that was almost palpable.

He wasn't Charles. It was a statement to herself, not a question. He wasn't her husband. She felt lightheaded, and for a moment she thought she'd pitch forward and down the rest of the stairs.

But then he moved toward her, stopping at the foot of the staircase. His eyes held hers, and Dupont might just as well not have been there. The world had narrowed to just the two of them. And as she stared at him, a shattering truth came to her. She'd known since the first time he touched her that he wasn't Charles.

She had to have known. As he held the banister, she remembered his touch on her. A stranger had been in her bed—an intimate stranger.

He took one step up. "I need to take care of this, Sean. Then I need to explain."

"Where's Charles Elliot?" Dupont cut in.

She stared at the man below her. The question echoed in her, yet she couldn't get out the words. Slowly she sank onto the step and slid her hand down the cool wood of one of the spindles. Should she scream, or call the police, or cry, or run? She couldn't do anything but stare.

As if he knew her thoughts, he took another step up and touched her knee where the robe parted. She jerked at the contact, shocked by the heat of his fingers and the sensations that his touch sent through her. "Please wait before you do anything."

She looked at his hand on her, and he drew back. Then she glanced up at him. It was true. He wasn't Charles. And it was true that she must have known from the first. For a moment she felt such shame that he could do this to her that she thought she was going to be sick. But as she swallowed, she was moved by an amazing sense of calm. It was the strange, unexplainable knowledge that she loved this man. He wasn't Charles, and she loved him. She couldn't move or speak as the stunning revelation became a reality to her.

She managed to nod—it was little more than a jerky motion of her head—and he exhaled unsteadily.

"Thank you," he whispered, then turned and went back down to Dupont. "Mr. Dupont, we'll talk. You and me."

"No, I—"

"You and me," the stranger said, then motioned to the library to the left of the doors. "In there."

The thin man hesitated, then shrugged and muttered, "I'd better get some answers," before he turned and walked toward the library.

When Sean saw the two men walking away, she got to her feet and found she could stand without support. She slowly went down the stairs and into the library. As she stopped at the doorway of the book-lined room, with its leather chairs and its chess table set up by the window, she knew that whatever happened, she would defend this man who could never really be a stranger to her.

Mac saw Sean step into the room. The paleness that had touched her face as the truth came to her was still there. She knew the truth, but she was holding herself together, clasping her hands tightly in front of her, and standing very straight just inside the door.

He looked at Paul Dupont. This wasn't the way he wanted to tell her, and certainly not the way he wanted her to find out about what her husband had attempted to do to the company. But it was out of his hands now. And as his stomach knotted, he knew this was all over. It was gone. And in that moment he knew that the memories would never be enough for him.

He went to the windows and glanced out to see a dark sedan parked behind the company car. Would it have been different if they had closed the gates? If they had ignored the door chimes and the knocks? No. He'd been around enough to know that when things happened, they happened for a reason. Dupont's arrival was just the means to an end.

"All right," he said as he turned his back on the windows and faced Dupont, who was in the middle of the room. "Tell me why you're here."

"That's between Elliot and me."

"It's between you and *me*. You're in this house. You came all the way from Paris. You talked to me on the phone repeatedly, and I want to know what's going on."

He threw his hands up. "I give up. All right. I don't know if you're his brother or what, but Charles Elliot owes me, and he's trying to blow me off. He can't. I know too much."

And the pieces of the puzzle fell into place for Mac. Dupont was in Accounting; he'd gotten a huge raise. Either he'd known what Charles was up to or he'd been in on it from the first. "Blackmail?"

The man's face flushed beet red. "No. Payment."

"You think because there's two and a half million dollars floating around, you deserve your cut?"

He heard Sean's sharp intake of air, but he didn't look at her. Dupont looked shocked. "What do you know about that?"

"Everything. Charles Elliot was bleeding the company, putting that money into a Swiss account, using the name Sidney Evans. My only question for you is how involved you were in the embezzlement."

The room was so silent that Mac could hear each breath each person took. He flashed a look at Sean, by the doors. The paleness remained, and her eyes were wide. "I found the money in an account in Geneva. There's a one-way ticket to Geneva for one Sidney Evans for a week from today. And this man—" he motioned to Dupont "—either was electronically funneling the money out, or he found out about it and was blackmailing Charles."

Sean stood very still. Mac's desire to hold her was overwhelming, but he had no right to do that. Not now. He looked away from her, toward Dupont. "Bad news, Paul. The money was taken out of the account today and transferred back into the company's general fund. I know you're familiar with the general fund. The account in Geneva is empty. You're out of luck."

Dupont looked as if he was going to have a seizure. Then he sputtered, "Oh, no, you don't! I don't know what this scam is, but I'm owed money, and I want it." He looked at Sean. "Don't you think the board of directors would be fascinated by a story about the daughter of the owner using an impostor for her husband, and both of them playing with the books?"

Mac stepped closer to Dupont. "How about the police being told about a man who's trying to blackmail a prominent Seattle family, a man who had a hand in embezzling millions, a man who—"

Dupont cut him off. "Hey, just a minute. I just want what's mine. I didn't take any money from the company, but I was promised a bonus if—"

"If you kept your mouth shut?" Mac demanded.

Sean abruptly turned to leave the room. God, it really was over, Mac thought. She was going to call the police. Dupont wouldn't be the only one in jail when they came. And Mac's first instinct was to get the hell out of town. But he couldn't. He couldn't leave like this, and he couldn't leave without making sure that Sean understood.

"I kept my part of the bargain," Dupont said, but his voice was lower now. "I made plans."

Mac looked at the man. "We all make plans, but that doesn't make them reality." He knew that so well. "It looks as if Charles Elliot has the last laugh on everyone."

"Mr. Dupont?"

Sean came back into the room with something in her hand. As she crossed to the chess table, Mac wondered if the police were on the way. She sat in one of the two chairs by the window and looked at Dupont. "Just how much money did my husband offer you?"

He hesitated, looking at Mac, then back at Sean. "Two hundred and fifty thousand."

She sat back, and Mac could see that she had a pen and a checkbook with her. She laid the book on the table and opened it, then began to write. "I think one hundred thousand dollars would be pretty fair compensation for not going to prison." She wrote quickly, then tore it from the book. "Don't you think so, Mr. Dupont?" she asked as she stood.

"But, I...I..."

She crossed to the man. "*Don't* you?"

He looked at her, then at Mac and back to the check in Sean's outstretched hand.

Mac moved closer to Sean. She was letting Dupont off the hook. "If I was you, I'd take it and run and never look back."

Dupont was motionless for a long moment, but then he reached for the check. When he tried to take it, Sean held on to it. "The deal is that what's been said in this room will go no further than these four walls."

"Of course," he said quickly.

"Your position at Warren International is terminated. This is severance pay, in case anyone asks. Agreed?"

Dupont nodded. "Agreed." And Sean let go of the check.

Mac moved toward the foyer. "It's time to leave, Mr. Dupont."

When he got to the entry doors, the man was right behind him. As he opened the barrier, Mac said, "And if you ever do anything to harm that lady, you'll have to answer to me."

He ducked his head and hurried out, quickly going down the steps. Mac watched until the car disappeared behind the gates. When the taillights faded into the night, he stepped back, closed the door and turned. Sean was right behind him.

Goodbye had never been part of his vocabulary. Walking away silently was the way he had always ended things in the past. But all that had changed. He stood there, looking at her in silence, wishing he could just kiss her one more time, but knowing he couldn't ever touch her again.

"You shouldn't have paid him off," he found himself saying. The words were so far from what was going on his mind that it surprised him.

"I didn't want the company to suffer. It would have been cheap at twice the price."

He understood. The company came first, even before justice. "What now?"

She bit her lip, and then he heard her take a shaky breath. "Where's Charles?"

He flinched internally at the question. "I told you about the accident, when I hit my head."

She fidgeted with the tie on her robe, winding the strip of terry cloth around and around her forefinger. Her eyes were wide, and overly bright. "He's dead, isn't he?"

He couldn't do anything but nod.

She didn't do a thing for a second. Then she closed her eyes and exhaled. "I guess I knew," she whispered.

"He was killed by a hit-and-run driver and he died instantly. I met him in a bar, and..." She opened her eyes and he could see the tears in them, waiting to fall. She might not have loved the man, but it was hurting her to hear all this. "He was on his way back here."

"To get his money."

"To take care of things, I guess."

"You look so much like him."

"They say everyone has a double, and he was mine." He spread his hands. "I can't explain why I did what I did, but... I saw him there, and he had everything. I didn't have anything. I saw your picture in his wallet, and I was drinking, and it seemed so simple. To just come here and be him."

She shook her head. "I can't believe this."

"They thought he was me."

A single tear slipped down her cheek. "Just who are you?"

Mac instinctively went to Sean, but stopped short of touching her. He looked down at her. "A liar, a con man, a manipulator. And a man who's more sorry than you'll ever know."

He could see the unsteadiness in her lower lip. "But you made things right for the company."

"One good point among so many rotten ones," he breathed.

She reached out to him. The touch of her fingers on his cheek was so unsteady that it broke his heart. "I don't even know your name."

"Mac."

"Mac," she whispered.

The sound of his name on her lips was as stunning as anything he'd heard in his life. The sound of it rang in his heart. Something to add to the memories. Maybe if he had enough of them, they would become substantial enough to hold off the horrible loneliness he knew was waiting for him when he walked out the door.

He touched her hand, closing his fingers around it. "I never expected things to be like they were. I thought Charles Elliot had a wife and a home and a business and friends. And I found out he had never been a real husband, he didn't want a home, he was destroying the business, and he was willing to leave everything and everyone for money."

She tried to lace her fingers through his, but he drew back. Being close was bad enough, but feeling her holding on to him was more than he could take. He put his hands behind his back. He had very little time before he had to go. "The man wasted his life."

"I knew you weren't Charles," she said as she pushed her hands in the pockets of her robe.

The statement astounded him. "You what?"

"I mean, I thought you were Charles." She shrugged—a fluttery movement of her slender shoulders. "But I think I knew in some part of me that you couldn't be Charles. He never cared about anything but himself. He would never have helped set up the tents, or worried about the business, or told Sandi Dunn to get lost. He would never have been able to knock those three guys around. And he could never have..." Her voice trailed off as high color dotted her cheeks.

"What couldn't he ever have done?"

"Made love to me like you did."

He was bombarded with the images of their love-making. "What a fool he was," Mac breathed.

"This is all crazy. You look like Charles. I mean, everyone seemed to believe you were Charles. Not that anyone around here really knew him. But it's like the world's gone mad."

"It's been mad for a very long time. But I'll do what I can to help set things right."

"You got the money back, and—"

"No, not that. I should have let Charles die when he did, instead of coming here to complicate things. You would have had him out of your life. It would have been over."

"But you are here, and you are Charles Elliot to everyone else."

A hollow lie. A lie he would have jumped at just days ago, but now it wasn't enough. "Charles needs to be dead. You need to get on with your life."

"But you—?"

"I don't belong here. I never did."

He didn't know quite what he expected, but it wasn't the tears that ran silently down her cheeks, or her words. "Yes, you do. You belong here more than Charles ever did."

"And another Dupont will show up at the door, and he won't be bought off. What then?"

"We...we can figure it out. It can work. It's worked for four days. It can work for four years. For a lifetime."

He wished it were true. He wished he could settle into the world of Charles Elliot and never look back. He had thought he could, but he'd been wrong. Dead wrong. "You don't even know who I am. Where I came from. What I was before all this."

"I want to know all those things." She swallowed hard. "But there is one thing I already know for sure. I love you, whoever you are."

He felt the words ringing in the air, flaring around him the way the fireworks had on the Fourth. Yet the truth dulled it. "You love a lie, an impostor."

She came to him then, gently touching his chest with her hands, and the contact was riveting. "I love *you*, Mac."

Loving her had been one thing, but to hear her say those words was almost his undoing. Mac kept his hands behind him, willing himself not to hold on to her for dear life. "Mackenzie Gerard," he whispered.

Chapter Thirteen

Mac held on to Sean while she slept for hours after they made love. He went over and over in his mind what he had to do, and as dawn began to invade the bedroom and rain to softly touch the windowpanes, he knew it was time to leave. He touched her hair with his lips, inhaled her scent as if he could stamp it on his soul, and then he let her go and eased himself out of bed.

He stood for a long moment, just looking at her, as she settled on her side with a sigh. Her hair was spread out on the pillow, and her face was gentle and beautiful, with her dark lashes grazing her cheekbones. If he left, he knew, he might never be able to come back—but this was his only chance of setting everything right.

He picked up the clothes he'd discarded, then turned and left without looking back. He went to Charles's room and dressed in Levi's, running shoes and a white T-shirt. Then he grabbed a windbreaker of Charles and slipped it on and crossed to the bed. He sorted through the drawer in the nightstand and found a piece of stationery and a pen.

He wrote quickly, then folded the paper in half and wrote "Sean" across it before lying it on the pillow of the undisturbed bed.

Then he stood and left the room, not looking at the closed doors of the master bedroom, and hurried down the stairs. He took nothing except the clothes and the briefcase, wallet and key chain the man had tossed to him that first night. Easing open the front door, he took one look up the staircase, then stepped outside. Dawn was just arriving, its gray light filtered through the soft summer rain, and the air smelled fresh and clean.

He got into the company car, started it, then drove away from the house. He went down the drive and through the open gates and turned to go down the hill. When he got to the bluffs, just past where Sean's car was parked, he gunned the engine and aimed at the side of the road, where it fell away to the water. At the last second he braked hard and laid rubber on the wet asphalt.

He backed up, and then, with the car in neutral, he rolled up the floor mat and jammed the accelerator down with it. He opened the briefcase, took out the plane ticket and tore it into little pieces, leaving the briefcase in the car. Then he took a hundred dollars out of Elliot's wallet and stuffed it in his pocket, along with the torn paper. As the engine roared, he scrambled out, shoved the gearshift into drive, and sent the car sailing forward.

The sedan crashed through the trees, tearing a path in its wake. The next instant, it disappeared from sight over the edge of the bluffs.

Mac walked through the path of broken plants and trees to the edge of the bluff. With rain on his face, he saw the car far below, nosedown in the dark, rain-stirred waters. As he watched, the back end sank until just the back bumper was visible, with bubbles foaming up around it. Then Mac took Charles's wallet out of his pocket and threw it at the car. It arced through the rain, then fell in the water within a few feet of the partially submerged car.

Charles Elliot was finally dead.

The rain came down harder as Mackenzie Gerard turned away from the sight and went back to the road to start down the hill toward the ferry landing. He didn't know how long it would take, but he had to go back to New Orleans, and Sean didn't have any part in that. It had to be settled before he could come back to Sanctuary Island . . . if he could ever come back.

SEAN WAS PULLED from a sweet, deep sleep by a knocking on the door. It took her a second or so to figure out where she was and that the knocking was on the bedroom door, not the entry door downstairs. She shifted in bed, reaching for Mac, but all she felt was the coolness of the linen.

When she opened her eyes and looked around, she was alone. Pushing herself up, she called out, "Come in," as she tugged the sheets up to cover herself.

The door clicked open, and Helen came into the bedroom dressed in white jeans and a neon pink T-shirt with Single And NOT Available! scrawled on it in gold.

"You must have the ringer off on the phone," Helzen called. "It's your father on the line."

"Thanks. Would you tell my...my husband that I need to talk to him?"

"I haven't seen him since I got here."

She held tightly to the sheet. "Maybe he's gone for a walk on the beach," she said, but something in her tightened. She couldn't sense his presence at all. It was as if a vacuum surrounded her.

Helen came across to the bed and held something out to Sean. "I found this note for you in his room."

Sean took the folded sheet of paper, then asked, "What time is it?"

"Just after nine."

The ferry had been running since early this morning, every fifteen minutes—a lot of chances to get clear of the island. "Thanks."

She waited until Helen had left, then unfolded the paper. She didn't know Mac's handwriting, but she could tell he'd written the note. The writing was more a scrawl than script, but easy to read, and she knew she was right, knew he was gone even before she read the words.

Sean, I can't stay in this lie. There are things that have to be settled, things I can't involve you in. Trust me on this, and don't do anything until you hear from the police. If I can, I'll find you again. Someway, somehow, no matter what, I'll be there. I love you. Mac

She stared at the painfully white sheet of paper, then

slowly folded it and held it in her hand. There were no tears, just a stinging in her eyes, and a loneliness in her heart that was a physical pain. She'd just learned what love was, and then love had been snatched away from her.

She jerked when another knock sounded on the bedroom door. She had to swallow twice before she could say, "Yes?"

"Your father's still waiting on the line," Helen called through the wood. "He says it's very important."

"Thanks," she murmured, then reached for the phone. "Louis?"

"Thank God. I didn't know what was going on."

"What's the emergency?" she asked, sinking back against the headboard and closing her eyes, feeling completely numb.

"It's over, Sean. It's over."

He knew! "Over?"

"The money was found in the general fund. I don't know how or why, but it's there. A lump sum, deposited yesterday afternoon."

She exhaled. "That's wonderful."

"You sound as if it's the end of the world. What's wrong?"

"I..." She bit her lip. "Dad, I need to take a break."

"Sean, what's going on?"

"I told you, I need to take a break."

"You called me Dad. It sounds as if your life's a bit off-center."

She felt the tears then, hot and scalding and silent, running down her cheek. Off-center? Life was upside down. "It is, I guess."

"What's Charles done?"

She tasted the salty tears on her lips. "Nothing. Nothing at all."

"Then what's happening with you? If it's the business, it's finished. There isn't a reason in the world to go public with what happened, and eventually we'll find out who did it. Don't worry about it. Warren International is still standing."

But she wasn't still standing. She felt as if her props had been snatched out from under her. "That's good. I'm happy about that."

"Are you going to come into the office today?"

She made herself open her eyes when she began to see images of Mac in her mind. Rain beat against the windows, and a wind was beginning to grow. "It's storming again. I'm going to stay at the house today."

"Is Charles coming in?"

"No, he's not."

"Sean, I want to talk to you about Charles. I've been thinking that—"

"Later," she whispered. "I'll call you...tomorrow...and we'll talk." She hung the receiver back in the cradle at the same time Helen knocked on the door again.

"Ma'am, the police are downstairs. They'd like to talk to you."

Sean stared at the note, then pushed it under her pillow and made herself get up. Mac had said the police would come. "Tell them I'll be right there."

She reached for her robe and pushed her feet into her slippers, not even bothering to look at herself in the mirror. Wiping the moisture off her face, she left the bedroom and went to the staircase. She looked down at the foyer at two very wet and very serious-looking policemen who were standing awkwardly on the polished floor.

Through sheer willpower, she made herself go down, not touching the banister. The two men looked at her, their faces sober. "Mrs. Elliot?"

She stopped as she stepped onto the floor. "Yes."

"I'm sorry, ma'am, but I'm afraid we have some bad news."

She hugged her arms around herself. "Bad news?" she breathed.

"A local gentleman was on the beach near here this morning, and he came across a car that had gone off the bluffs. It hit the water and was barely visible."

"A car?"

"It was registered to your company, and when we contacted them they said it was being used by your husband, Charles Elliot." The man came closer, his face filled with concern. "I'm sorry, ma'am, but I'm afraid it looks like he went out of control and over the edge of the bluffs into the water. We haven't been able to find his . . . him."

"What?"

"Well, there's a slim chance that he got out and we'll find him."

She sank down on the bottom step, and the tears came back. It was over. Charles was really dead. Mac had seen to it. "He . . . he's dead."

"Is there someone we could call for you, someone to help you?"

She looked up at the man, whose image was blurred by her tears. "My husband couldn't swim."

The man hunkered down in front of her, his fingers gripping the wet cap in his hands. "Ma'am, we should call someone."

She shook her head. "He's dead," she whispered. "It's over." And the last thing she knew before she fainted was that Mac was gone. He hadn't stayed after all.

December 24

MAC INHALED the freshness of the ocean air as he got out of the tractor-trailer that had given him a ride from Walla Walla, Washington, into Seattle. He stood alone on the street in a cold wind that cut through his denim clothes.

He was back. He was close to home. He set off at a fast walk to go down the hills to the docking area to get the ferry for Sanctuary Island.

It was the path he'd taken the first time, when fate had grabbed him by the collar and jerked him into another man's life. Now he was back, as Mackenzie Gerard, and he wanted his own life.

He caught sight of himself in the windows of the stores he passed. He looked like a man who had been on the road for a long time. A man with hair long enough to lay on the collar of his denim jacket. A man with a mustache and the stubble of a three-day beard. A man who looked a little like the late Charles Elliot.

By the time he reached the ferry landing, a misty rain had begun to fall. He'd first come here in the rain, and he had left in the rain. It seemed appropriate to be stepping onto the deck of the ferry and feeling the rain on his face again. He passed the guard he'd talked to on the first trip, Marvin, but the man didn't acknowledge him.

Mac paid his fare, then moved to the railing. As the ferry began to ease out of the channel, Mac looked out at the island in the distance. He was surprised when someone touched his shoulder, and he turned to find Marvin at his side. "There's a nice warm place inside, out of the rain, if you'd like."

Mac shook his head, not caring that the rain was beginning to seep under his collar. "Thanks. I like it outside."

Marvin studied him intently. "You know, you sort of look familiar. Have you ever lived on the island?"

"I did, quite a while ago."

"Thought so. I never forget a face. You been gone a while?"

"Yeah, too long."

"Where are you coming from?"

"New Orleans."

"A beautiful city, I hear."

"I didn't get a chance to see much of it." They'd dropped the accessory charges, but he'd been given a year's jail sentence, reduced to five months, for violating a court order and leaving the state. It had left

Mac with an aversion to anything that made him feel closed in. The moment he'd been let out, six days ago, he'd left New Orleans, and he hadn't looked back.

He glanced across the water at the island, which was coming closer now. "To tell you the truth, it's more beautiful here than it was there."

"I believe that." Marvin smiled. "You've been away too long."

"You've got that right."

"And what a good time to come back."

"How's that?"

"Christmas. Tomorrow's the big day."

Mac smiled. He'd forgotten all about holidays. All he'd worried about was the time he had left, and what was happening to Sean. Through the papers he'd kept track of her as best he could. He'd read the news about her husband's funeral, with a picture of her dressed in black with Louis at her side, and he'd seen in the financial pages that Warren International's stock had been one of the few to increase in value in the past quarter.

He'd kept a single clipping from the newspaper, a grainy photo of Sean that was almost falling apart from being carried in his wallet. "Christmas," he murmured. "I'm going home for Christmas."

Marvin slapped him on the shoulder. "Happy holidays," the man said, then moved off as the ferry approached the piling channel at the docking area on the island.

Mac stayed where he was until the ferry had come to a laborious halt at the dock and the safety chain had been undone. Then, as the cars inched off, he walked onto the dock and up the ramp onto Sanctuary Island.

He waited until the cars were out of the parking lot, and then he went past the cars waiting to board and headed for the road. He turned right and started up the incline to the top of the bluffs. *Home.* The word echoed in his mind, over and over again. *Home.*

At the curve in the road, he saw that the trees and brush had grown to cover the scars where the car had cut through them. He kept going upward. There were so many scars in life, and he had more than his share. He just hoped they would be covered when he got to the house.

As he approached the entrance to Ten Look Out Point, he walked up to the security gate and looked through the wrought-iron barrier at the house. For a second he almost turned away. He had lived for months with the hope that he and Sean could have a life together. But at that moment the thought that it might not happen came to him.

What if she wasn't even here anymore? What if she had moved on with her life? What if what had happened between them had been just a moment in time, instead of the start of a new life? He turned from the gates, but didn't leave. He had to know.

He went to the call box, and pushed the button. "Yes?" said a voice he recognized as Helen's.

"I'm here for Mrs. Elliot."

"That's Ms. Warren. And I'm afraid she's not here."

Mac had no idea what time it was. "When do you expect her?"

"I'm not sure when she'll return. Why don't you try back later on?"

Mac let go of the talk button. The rain was beginning to fall harder, but he knew he wasn't going anywhere. He spotted a large tree by the fence and walked toward it. He went under its spreading branches, and in the shelter it offered from the storm he leaned against the rough trunk and waited.

SEAN DROVE OFF THE FERRY just after five. With the rain falling steadily and the light of day failing rapidly, she snapped on her headlights as she started up the hill. When she came to the curve, she made herself look straight ahead. For so long she'd slowed and looked at the trees that had been broken and the brush that had been torn up.

Or she'd remembered when she'd run out of gas and Mac had found her with Jerry and his cronies. He'd rescued her like a knight in shining armor. She laughed at the thought, then sobered. That same knight had walked away from her and dropped off the face of the earth.

God knew she'd tried to find him. She'd found a handful of Mackenzie Gerards, but none of them was Mac. She'd even hired a discreet private investigator who had turned up nothing. The hit-and-run victim identified as Mackenzie Gerard had had little, if any, background. He'd moved around the country like a nomad. The address on the driver's license from New Jersey had been outdated and untraceable.

When Sean had arranged to take possession of the body, there had been few questions. And when she'd had it buried in Charles's plot, no one had been there but her. She approached the gate to the property and hit the opener. As the car idled while the gates opened, she caught a movement in the rain near the trees. But the window was blurred by the moisture. In the poor light, all she could make out was a shadow.

She hesitated before she drove through the open gate, and the next thing she knew someone walked to the front of her car. For an instant she saw a man caught in the glare of the headlights. Tall and lean, the man was soaked through. His dark hair was plastered to his head, and his denim clothes were dripping with rain. Yet he stood right in front of her car, just letting the rain fall.

Sean stared at him, at the angles and planes of his face in the bright light. There was a mustache, a scruffy beard, longer hair. Her heart began to race. The impossible was happening. A miracle. Mac had kept his word. He'd found her again.

She pushed the car into Park and opened the door. As the rain touched her, she didn't feel the cold or the wetness. All she was aware of was the man coming around the car. She'd waited for this forever. An eternity. Mac. She took a step toward him as the wind snatched the door and slammed it shut.

"Sean?" he said, his voice so familiar to her from her dreams that she'd had constantly since he left, and she knew she was crying.

"It's you," she breathed as he came closer.

For a long moment they stood a foot apart, rain and wind all around. Sean was afraid to move, in case the image disappeared into the rain. In case she was imagining something she wanted so desperately.

Then she saw him clearly, saw the uncertainty in his eyes, and she threw herself into his arms, holding on to him for dear life. Her tears were harsh sobs that racked her body, and he held her close to his heart. A time of darkness was over, and she felt as if her life had just begun.

"Mac," she whispered. "You came back."

He held her tightly against him, and his voice rumbled in her ears. "How could I not come back? I didn't have a life without you."

She didn't let go, but she eased back enough to look up at him. The blueness of his gaze held hers, and she touched his face with one hand, her fingers running over the bristle of beard. "Mackenzie Gerard."

"Yes, in person."

"You're beautiful."

"I think that's my line," he said, his voice vaguely unsteady.

"This never has been a traditional relationship, has it?"

He cupped her face with his hands, his thumbs smoothing away the rain and tears on her cheeks. "No, it never was. Maybe it never will be. But one very traditional thing I want to do is ask you to marry me."

She knew that people didn't die from excessive happiness, but for a moment she thought she might. And she couldn't think of a better place to die than in

Mac's arms. "Yes, I'll marry you, Mackenzie Gerard."

He bent to touch his lips to hers. The kiss was deep and searching, until Sean felt a peace in her heart that defied logic. Her soul settled into a bliss that gave way to a need that had been simmering for five months. At the same moment, Mac trailed his lips to her ear and whispered, "I love you, Sean."

She felt more tears come to mingle with the rain, and she could barely speak. "I love you, Mackenzie Gerard."

He drew back. "This is a new life, our life, and I want to start it as soon as we can."

"How about now?" she whispered, and kissed him again.

Epilogue

Mac woke to darkness and the heat of Sean by his side. A peace that he'd never known before seemed to fill him, and he knew he'd come home. Home hadn't been the island or even this house—it had been Sean all along. No matter where they were, if she was with him, he'd be home.

She stirred at his side, and then he heard her sigh. "Are you awake?" he asked.

"Mmm..." she murmured, shifting until her leg was over his thigh and her arm lay across his chest. "Sort of."

"I was just thinking that this is the first time I ever came home."

He could feel her shift to look at him, but he still stared at the shadows over the bed. "The first time?"

"I never had a home, not really. Foster homes, things like that, but not a place where I belonged."

She tapped his chest with her fingers. "You belong here, with me."

"I know I do. And I know it's not the house, it's you." He turned to face her, his hand lying on the swelling of her hip. "You, Sean, you're home for me."

She propped herself on her elbow and traced a feathery line with the tip of her finger along the angle of his shoulder. "Home? I like that. Being home. It sounds so...so right."

"It does, doesn't it?"

"Yes." Her finger rested at the hollow of his throat. "These past five months, I looked for you everywhere."

He knew he had to tell her. "I was in jail."

She didn't pull back or even give a gasp of surprise. "So, that's where you were hiding."

"I mean it, I was in jail." He told her about the trial, about his not showing up for court and having a warrant out for his arrest. And he told her about going back. "They gave me a year, and I served five months."

"That's why you wouldn't tell me what you had to do?"

"I didn't want you involved, and I sure as hell didn't want you being one of those women who file in on visiting day to see the inmates, no matter how long a time I had to serve. I didn't know what they were going to do, and I was lucky to get off so lightly."

"Five months was a very long time," she whispered, and he felt the trembling in her finger on him.

"An eternity," he conceded. "I never stopped thinking about you. I was worried, but I knew you'd understand what I did, and why."

"I did." She rested her hand over his heart, and he was sure she could feel it hammering against his ribs. "And Charles got his burial."

"Good. He deserved that much." He held her to him. "What about now? If I stay here, everyone's going to know what went on."

She touched his lips with the tips of her fingers. "No one will. They only see what they want to see. They'll meet you as Mackenzie Gerard, someone I met a while back, maybe five months or so. They pretty much knew Charles had his affairs, so they won't be too surprised if I had one." She exhaled softly. "And even if you look a bit like him, they'll think I'm lucky to find someone who doesn't act like him at all."

"That's asking a lot of people."

"Maybe. If we have to, we'll go someplace else."

"I don't have a job, or any real training."

"That's not true. You turned the company around. You saved it from ruin. We could certainly use you there."

"Will you be my boss?"

"Mmm . . . That has a nice ring to it," she said with a soft chuckle. "Being married has an even better ring to it."

"You're right. Let's get married quietly, then come back and see what happens here."

"That sounds like a good plan to me," she whispered.

"Does anyone know about the money?"

"Just Dad and me."

"Dad?"

"Yes, Dad."

"When did that start?"

"When I realized that family was everything. That having the people you loved around you was the most important thing in the world. It just seemed right to call him Dad, the way I used to when I was young."

"Does he know about me?"

"He knew from the start, I think. But he was willing to let it be if I was all right. A real father. They're like that, forgiving and kind, as long as their child is safe and happy."

"I wouldn't know," he said. "I don't remember my father at all."

She ran her hand over his chest, moving it downward. He found himself almost holding his breath. "That's a shame. I can't imagine being without mine. A child should have a father to be there no matter what, and to love them. Don't you think so?"

He trembled when she gently splayed her fingers on his abdomen. He hadn't thought he could need this woman any more than when he'd first laid eyes on her again. Rain-soaked clothes hadn't stopped them from falling into bed and taking each other with a passion and urgency that five months had fueled.

But as her hand moved on him, as he felt her hair lying soft against his skin, he knew that he wanted her more than ever. His hand eased her hips closer to him, and then he gently brushed her damp hair back from her temple. "It's great to have a father there for you. You're very lucky."

"I know I am," she whispered, and her hand moved lower still. When she found the evidence of a passion that couldn't be denied, he drew in an unsteady breath and closed his eyes. "Let me show you how lucky we both are."

She took his hand and held it against her, gently pressing it to her abdomen. He opened his eyes to look at her.

She was smiling. It was a secret sort of smile that gave a beauty to her face that took his breath away. Then she moved his hand on her, brushing his palm over her stomach and abdomen, across a gentle swelling that he'd overlooked in his urgency to have her.

"No," he whispered.

"Oh, yes."

Mac knew that luck had worked overtime for him, that fate had dealt him a hand that he finally wanted to keep. "You're pregnant?"

"*We* are pregnant, although I've been the one with morning sickness, and the one who hasn't been able to eat a decent meal in ages." Her smile faltered. "You're going to be a father, a good father, and you're always going to be there for our child, aren't you?"

He'd never thought about children, but the idea of a child of his and Sean's was so right. So overwhelming. "A child," he whispered. "Our child." He kissed her, a fierce kiss that seared into his soul. He wanted her, but he held back. "Is it all right to... to be together?"

She drew back and looked down at him, her laughter a wondrous thing in his ears. "I think it's a bit late to worry about that, don't you?" She moved closer. "And, yes, it's just fine for now. And tomorrow's Christmas. It sort of fits, doesn't it?"

He looked into her face, and it conjured up thoughts of real picnics, and a dog, and lots of Christmases, and lots of children. Sean's and his.

Sanctuary Island. It had given him sanctuary in the arms of this woman and the life they were going to have.

"It sure does fit," he whispered, and as he pulled her close, he knew he was holding the best Christmas present ever in his arms. "Merry Christmas."

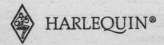 

My Valentine
1994

Celebrate the most romantic day of the year with
MY VALENTINE 1994
a collection of original stories, written by
four of Harlequin's most popular authors...

MARGOT DALTON
MURIEL JENSEN
MARISA CARROLL
KAREN YOUNG

*Available in February, wherever
Harlequin Books are sold.*

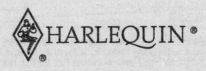
HARLEQUIN ®

VAL94

When the only time you have for yourself is...

Spring into spring—by giving yourself a March Break! Take a few *stolen moments* and treat yourself to a Great Escape. Relax with one of our brand-new stories (or with all six!).

Each STOLEN MOMENTS title in our Great Escapes collection is a complete and never-before-published *short* novel. These contemporary romances are 96 pages long—the perfect length for the busy woman of the nineties!

Look for Great Escapes in our Stolen Moments display this March!

SIZZLE by Jennifer Crusie
ANNIVERSARY WALTZ
by Anne Marie Duquette
MAGGIE AND HER COLONEL
by Merline Lovelace
PRAIRIE SUMMER by Alina Roberts
THE SUGAR CUP by Annie Sims
LOVE ME NOT by Barbara Stewart

Wherever Harlequin and Silhouette books are sold.

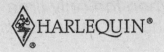

®HARLEQUIN®

MARRIAGE
BY *Design*

Harlequin proudly presents four stories about
convenient but not *conventional* reasons for marriage:

- ◆ To save your godchildren from a
  "wicked stepmother"

- ◆ To help out your eccentric aunt—and her sexy
  business partner

- ◆ To bring an old man happiness by making him
  a grandfather

- ◆ To escape from a ghostly existence and become a
  real woman

Marriage By Design—four brand-new stories by four
of Harlequin's most popular authors:

CATHY GILLEN THACKER
JASMINE CRESSWELL
GLENDA SANDERS
MARGARET CHITTENDEN

Don't miss this exciting collection of stories about
marriages of convenience. Available in April, wherever
Harlequin books are sold.

MBD94

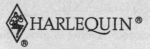

HARLEQUIN®

COMING SOON TO
A STORE NEAR YOU...

THE MAIN
ATTRACTION

By *New York Times* Bestselling Author

This March, look for THE MAIN ATTRACTION by popular
author Jayne Ann Krentz.

Ten years ago, Filomena Cromwell had left her small town
in shame. Now she is back determined to get her sweet,
sweet revenge....

Soon she has her ex-fiancé, who cheated on her with
another woman, chasing her all over town. And he isn't
the only one. Filomena lets Trent Ravinder catch her.

Can she control the fireworks she's set into motion?

HARLEQUIN®

Don't miss these Harlequin favorites by some of our most distinguished authors!
And now, you can receive a discount by ordering two or more titles!

HT#25409	THE NIGHT IN SHINING ARMOR by JoAnn Ross	$2.99 ☐
HT#25471	LOVESTORM by JoAnn Ross	$2.99 ☐
HP#11463	THE WEDDING by Emma Darcy	$2.89 ☐
HP#11592	THE LAST GRAND PASSION by Emma Darcy	$2.99 ☐
HR#03188	DOUBLY DELICIOUS by Emma Goldrick	$2.89 ☐
HR#03248	SAFE IN MY HEART by Leigh Michaels	$2.89 ☐
HS#70464	CHILDREN OF THE HEART by Sally Garrett	$3.25 ☐
HS#70524	STRING OF MIRACLES by Sally Garrett	$3.39 ☐
HS#70500	THE SILENCE OF MIDNIGHT by Karen Young	$3.39 ☐
HI#22178	SCHOOL FOR SPIES by Vickie York	▸$2.79 ☐
HI#22212	DANGEROUS VINTAGE by Laura Pender	$2.89 ☐
HI#22219	TORCH JOB by Patricia Rosemoor	$2.89 ☐
HAR#16459	MACKENZIE'S BABY by Anne McAllister	$3.39 ☐
HAR#16466	A COWBOY FOR CHRISTMAS by Anne McAllister	$3.39 ☐
HAR#16462	THE PIRATE AND HIS LADY by Margaret St. George	$3.39 ☐
HAR#16477	THE LAST REAL MAN by Rebecca Flanders	$3.39 ☐
HH#28704	A CORNER OF HEAVEN by Theresa Michaels	$3.99 ☐
HH#28707	LIGHT ON THE MOUNTAIN by Maura Seger	$3.99 ☐

Harlequin Promotional Titles

#83247	YESTERDAY COMES TOMORROW by Rebecca Flanders	$4.99 ☐
#83257	MY VALENTINE 1993	$4.99 ☐
	(short-story collection featuring Anne Stuart, Judith Arnold, Anne McAllister, Linda Randall Wisdom)	

(limited quantities available on certain titles)

	AMOUNT	$
DEDUCT:	10% DISCOUNT FOR 2+ BOOKS	$
ADD:	POSTAGE & HANDLING	$
	($1.00 for one book, 50¢ for each additional)	
	APPLICABLE TAXES*	$ _____
	TOTAL PAYABLE	$ _____
	(check or money order—please do not send cash)	

To order, complete this form and send it, along with a check or money order for the total above, payable to Harlequin Books, to: **In the U.S.:** 3010 Walden Avenue, P.O. Box 9047, Buffalo, NY 14269-9047; **In Canada:** P.O. Box 613, Fort Erie, Ontario, L2A 5X3.

Name: _____

Address: _____ City: _____

State/Prov.: _____ Zip/Postal Code: _____

*New York residents remit applicable sales taxes.
Canadian residents remit applicable GST and provincial taxes.

HBACK-JM